Puffin Books
Editor: Kaye

The Chesterfie

Robert G. Chesterfield was an eccentric. When he sent
money from the United States to found a new children's
hospital in England, he sent it in the form of one hundred
and four gold ingots, all stamped with his initials. Each
gold bar weighed about twenty pounds and was worth some
four thousand pounds.

But the gold never reached London. Despite all the plans for
guarding it, a gang managed to rob the train, and disappear
without trace.

Chief-superintendent Branxome of Scotland Yard, who was
put in charge of the investigation, believed it was virtually
impossible to smuggle the gold out of England, and every
boat and aeroplane that left the country was carefully
searched.

But some of the gold turned up in Paris and it was his
own children who discovered the first clue, on their way to
France for a family holiday in their boat, the *Dabchick*. It
led to thrilling adventures for Peter, Jill and Michael as
they trailed a suspicious craft through the harbours of
Normandy and up the Seine to Paris.

Masses of action and excitement for readers of nine and over.

Cover design by Barbara Nunan

Roger Pilkington

The Chesterfield Gold

Illustrated by Piet Klaasse

Penguin Books

Penguin Books Ltd, Harmondsworth,
Middlesex, England
Penguin Books Inc., 7110 Ambassador Road,
Baltimore, Maryland 21207, U.S.A.
Penguin Books Australia Ltd, Ringwood,
Victoria, Australia

First published by Macmillan 1957
Published in Puffin Books 1968
Reprinted 1971
Copyright © Roger Pilkington, 1957

Made and printed in Great Britain by
Cox & Wyman Ltd,
London, Reading and Fakenham
Set in Monotype Baskerville

To Hugh
and all young people
who can handle a boat

Contents

1   A Midsummer Night   9
2   Message from Paris   24
3   Tea and the Compass   39
4   Down on the Keel   60
5   Michael Gets Busy   79
6   A Misunderstanding at Night   99
7   Discovery at the Lock   122
8   What the Squid Did   147
9   Statue of Liberty   168

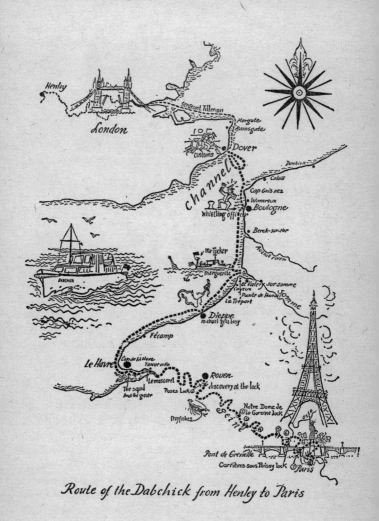

Henley
London
Sergeant Tillman
Margate
Ramsgate
Customs
Dover
Channel
Dunkirk
Colais
Cap Gris nez
Wimereux
Boulogne
whistling off!
Berck-sur-mer
Authie river
Mr Tucker
Marguerite
St Valery sur Somme
Cayeux
Pointe de Hourdel
Le Tréport
Dieppe
Michael gets busy
Somme
Fécamp
DABCHICK
Cap de la Here
Tancarville
Le Havre
Lemascaret
Rouen
discovery at the lock
The squid
And the grocer
Poses Lock
Notre Dame de
la Garenne lock
crayfishes
Seine
Pont de Grenelle
Carrières sous Poissy lock
Paris

Route of the Dabchick from Henley to Paris

1. A Midsummer Night

'Where are we, Daddy?' Michael half-opened his eyes as he lay back in the front seat of the car. It was after dark and the sodium street lamps overhead flooded the inside of the car with intermittent flashes of orange light.

'This is Salisbury,' answered his father. 'Go to sleep again. You've had a long day.'

'I'm not sleepy,' Michael said, trying to hide a big yawn which contradicted his words. 'But it must be quite late.'

'It's nearly midnight. I hope your mother and Jill won't be worried about us. I said they could expect us home by twelve, but it doesn't look as though we shall be there before about two in the morning. Still, you can lie in bed tomorrow as it's Saturday and there's no school.' He slowed down as they approached a fork in the road. Basingstoke was marked to the right, and a little way ahead the street lights came to an end.

'These school functions are always the same,' he continued. 'There are speeches to thank the cast and the producer and the stage manager and the chap who fixed up the amplifier for the music in the interval, and then of course there are refreshments . . .'

'They were super, too,' put in Michael.

'. . . and by the time you've shaken hands with the headmaster and asked the classics master how Peter's Latin is getting along it's half-past ten. Still, I'm glad we went.'

'So am I,' agreed Michael. 'I loved it where Peter stabbed himself. "Farewell, friends; thus Thisby ends. Adieu, adieu, adieu."' He giggled. 'He came down a terrific crash on the stage. I think it must be super to act in a decent play like *A Midsummer Night's Dream*. We always have such soppy ones at our school – you know, Robin Hood and his Merry Men and that sort of stuff. And Jill's seems just the same, only they have those boring historical things too, all about Anne Boleyn or Queen Elizabeth. I suppose it's easier for them because the characters are all women.'

Chief-superintendent Branxome laughed. 'I expect you'll act some better plays one day. Anyway, Peter did well tonight and so did the whole cast. I'm sorry your mother and Jill weren't there, but it always seems that we have to split up because Jill and Peter both have school functions on the same days. What people do if they have a really big family all having speech days and half-terms at the same moment I can't imagine.'

'I'm glad I came with you to Peter's,' said Michael. 'Jill's would have been all right, but all those exhibitions of sewing and cookery and things are a bit boring. Not as much fun as a play, anyway.' He yawned again. 'Of course, it's really best when we can all be together.'

'And that's not until the holidays. Only four weeks more.'

'Five and two days. Jill breaks up late.'

'Five and a bit then. We'll have to be thinking about what we're going to do this summer.'

'It's all very well thinking, Daddy,' said Michael doubtfully. 'We often have lovely plans of what we're going to do in the holidays, and then just when we're ready to go something happens and Scotland Yard say they're very sorry but they want you to stay behind and take over the case. It seems to happen nearly every time.'

His father sighed. What Michael said was true enough. Big cases always seemed to crop up at awkward moments, and several times he had had to cut short his holiday and return to the Yard to deal with them.

'I'm afraid crooks don't take time off, Michael. That's the trouble. And so long as they're on the go I have to be ready to take charge of the cases. I'm sorry, but it can't be helped. I can't just say I won't help to solve them.'

'No,' said Michael rather doubtfully. 'I suppose you can't.'

Michael was proud of the fact that Scotland Yard relied on his father to take over all the really important and difficult cases, but it annoyed him if they interfered with the holidays. 'I mean, I just hope there won't be anything to upset the holidays this time,' he said.

'I don't think there will. What would you like to do this summer?'

'Let's go somewhere exciting, Daddy. Somewhere we've never been before.'

'We could go away with the car somewhere.'

'Yes. Or in the boat. I think the boat is more fun. If we went in the car we would have to stay in some stuffy old hotel.'

'It might not be stuffy,' said his father. 'It might be one down by the sea somewhere, or even abroad.'

'I suppose it might,' agreed Michael reluctantly. 'But if we want to go to the sea the *Dabchick* is even better. We can go right on the sea in her. And abroad too.'

'That's true. Anyway, we'll do something that everybody likes. Your mother and I will have to think seriously about it soon. Meanwhile, how about a bit more sleep?'

And this time Michael did doze off. It was not very comfortable trying to sleep in the front of the car, but the hum of the engine seemed to help, and soon he was sound asleep whilst his father drove on across Wiltshire into Hampshire and towards home.

When Michael next awoke forty minutes later it was because of the scream of the brakes as his father pulled up quickly. He sat up at once and stared blankly at what he saw. In the road, only a few yards ahead of the car, a weird-looking individual was shown up in the headlights, his jacket torn, his trousers dirty and ragged, and his hair dishevelled and half over his eyes. The man was not waving the car to stop but was limping awkwardly towards them with his hands behind his back. Round the lower part of his face a dark woollen scarf was bound like a smog mask. His curious gait was due to his having no shoes or socks.

'Daddy, what on earth . . .'

Just at that moment the man turned round, and they saw that his wrists were tied tightly across each other with a piece of stout cord. ..

'Stay in the car,' said Mr Branxome almost sharply. 'It may be a trick.' He jumped out, ran up to the man, and pulled down the scarf from his face so that it hung round his neck, where it would serve as a useful handle if necessary. And, as the man's face came into full view in the lights of the car, Michael's father let out a gasp.

'It's Denby!'

The man was half dazzled by the glare of the headlights, but when he heard his name spoken by a familiar voice he stared in astonishment.

'Good heavens, sir, it's you!' But he didn't waste time in asking how his chief-superintendent had suddenly appeared on the scene in the middle of the night and out in the wilds of Hampshire. That could all wait. It was enough that Mr Branxome of all people was there.

'If you'll free my hands, sir,' he said in a quieter voice, 'we shall need to get to a telephone right away, and . . .'

'Michael!'

'Yes, Daddy?' He opened the door of the car.

'Quick, come here, and bring your knife.'

As Mr Branxome began carefully to saw into the cord with the knife blade, Michael stood and stared, still hardly able to believe that he was not dreaming what he saw. What he heard seemed hardly more real as the man panted it out in short sentences between gasps for breath.

'The bullion, sir. They stopped the train. Attacked the van and got the better of me. Cleared off in a lorry with the lot. Got its number, sir, DN 8716.'

'Write it down, Michael.' Mr Branxome gave a grunt of satisfaction as the cord parted. 'There, that's better.' He unwound the coils and put the cord in his pocket.

'How long ago did all this happen, Denby?'

'Must be nearly an hour since they got clear, sir.' Denby pointed to his feet. 'They took my shoes and socks to delay me, no doubt.'

'Clever idea, that,' put in the chief-superintendent. 'I've never come across that dodge before. Are your feet sore?'

'Not too bad, sir. A bit scratched perhaps. It's a rough track I had to come down to reach the main road.'

'Are you all right otherwise? You look rather knocked about.'

'I'm all right,' Denby replied with an attempt at a smile. 'I had a little rough-and-tumble, of course, but they put me under with a whiff of chloroform –'

'If you're all right then we had better get moving,' Mr Branxome interrupted. 'There's a phone-box at the fork a couple of miles back. I'll phone the County men at Stockbridge, give them the number of the lorry, and get things moving. Then we'll deal with the details.' He jumped into the car as Denby scrambled into the back, followed by Michael. Turning quickly round, he drove off fast down the road.

'Carry on, Denby. Give us the details.'

'The place is about three-quarters of a mile up a rough track, leading off the road a couple of hundred yards beyond where you met me, sir.' As Denby spoke he was working to untie the scarf that hung loose round his neck. Michael got to work on the knot and managed to untie it.

'I'll take the scarf if you don't mind,' said Denby, folding it carefully and putting it in his pocket. 'It might be a handy clue.'

'How long were you unconscious?' asked Mr Branxome without taking his eyes off the road.

'I don't know, sir. When I came round I was lying by the railway line and they were fastening up the back of the lorry. I thought it best to lie quiet and observe what I could, sir.' Denby's voice sounded as though he feared that this might be taken for cowardice, but Mr Branxome quickly put him at his ease.

'Quite right. Not much point in making a scene if you're tied up and gagged. Could you recognize the men again?'

'I doubt it, sir, what with the dark and the trees alongside the railway line –'

'Never mind. How many were there?'

'Five, sir.'

'And you were alone? You hadn't much of a chance, then.'

'No, sir. I gave one or two of them a bit of a belting though, before they got me fixed up.'

'What about the lorry? What sort was it?'

'I only saw the rear, sir. It was a big furniture lorry. I should say it was dark green with double doors and a tail-board.'

'At least we've got the number of the thieves' lorry,' said Michael. 'That should make it easy to find out who they were.'

'I doubt it,' commented his father. 'I don't imagine they were fools enough to use their own lorry. Ten to one it's stolen, and false number plates too. If they're smart enough to take Sergeant Denby's shoes and socks, they won't slip up on a number plate.'

The road swung left, and there at the fork ahead was the phone-box. Mr Branxome drew up quickly and all three jumped out, but the box was locked.

'Confound it,' muttered Michael's father. 'You have to be a club member and have a key. This is no time to start wondering about joining clubs. The Home Office will have to give them a new door, that's all.' And he flung himself against the phone-box with all the weight of his fifteen stone. At his third attack there was a splitting sound and the upper half of the door parted. Wrenching out the boards he leaned in and lifted the receiver.

'Give me the police at Stockbridge. Quickly please – it's an emergency call. No, I can't tell you what number this is,' he said abruptly. 'It's a road-box phone somewhere. It's pitch dark, man, how can I look and see? Oh, we'll see about all that later.' He hummed impatiently. 'Got the number of the lorry, Michael?'

'Yes, Daddy. DN 8716.'

'Thanks. Hello, hello, police? Chief-superintendent Branxome speaking, Flying Squad. Listen. Get all stations alerted over the whole county to stop a large dark lorry, pantechnicon type, DN 8716. Yes, D for Donald, N for Nothing. Eight, seven, that's right, one, six. Probably five men in it. Yes, big stuff too. Robbed a whole van load of bullion off the railway. About half a million pounds, that's all. It was landed from the *Ascania* at Southampton this evening. Good. Right. Just a moment.' He withdrew his head from the box. 'What is it, Denby?'

'The van is still on the line, sir. They had better get on to the railway and hold up traffic in case it should be run down. It has two red lights on it, but you never know.'

'Quite right.' Mr Branxome turned to the telephone again and passed on the information. 'And just one or two things more. Get plenty of men sent up here from County Head-quarters. Photographers, finger-prints and the whole shooting match. Got that? Right. I shall wait for them here at the fork. Goodness knows, but it's six or seven miles out of

Stockbridge on the Basingstoke road, with a phone-box at the junction. Ah; you know it, do you? Good.

'Oh, and send up a first-aid kit. No, nothing serious, just a few scratches. And get hold of a pair of socks and some shoes or boots or something. I don't care where you get them from. And phone up the Yard and tell them to ring my wife and say we're detained and won't be back till morning. Me and my son. Mrs Branxome, yes. They've got my number.' He hung up.

'Look here, Daddy,' said Michael curiously as they sat in the car waiting, 'I don't see how you knew that there was all that gold, and where it had come from and everything. Mr Denby didn't tell you.'

His father laughed. 'I just happened to know, that's all. When Denby said they had robbed a train of a load of bullion I didn't need to ask which train and whose gold. It's not often there's a shipment that size going about. Besides, I had seen the plans put up by the Bank of England for moving the stuff, and thought them foolproof. Amongst other things, I knew that my old friend Sergeant Denby was to sit in with the gold all the way up to London. We're old friends, aren't we, Denby?'

'That's right, sir. We've been on some good jewel robberies together.'

'And this looks like being one of the best yet, and by a piece of luck I was here on the spot instead of being hauled down from a good night's sleep up in London. Do you think that's a good omen, Michael?'

'It might be, Daddy. I hope you catch the thieves, and then – well, in a way, I hope you don't. I think bullion robberies are rather fun.'

'Rather fun, eh? What d'you think of that, Denby, from a boy born and bred in Scotland Yard traditions?'

Denby laughed. 'I'm not sure he's not right, sir. I might have ended up that way myself if I hadn't joined the force. There's a bit of sport in big-scale stuff like this job, no matter which side you're on.'

'Besides,' added Michael, grateful for this support, 'if you steal gold you're not pinching anything that matters. Mr Gregson was telling us about gold and banks in the civics lesson on Tuesday. He said, "Gold is a purely conventional sign of no value in itself, representing an imaginary foundation for a financial structure based on worthless pieces of paper." So there!'

'Well,' commented his father, 'all I can say is it's a good job your Mr Gregson is a schoolmaster and not a C.I.D. officer. I wouldn't choose to walk into the Bank of England and tell them that the day after they've lost this little lot. But in any case, he's wrong this time. The gold represents more than an imaginary foundation for nothing at all. Now you're mixed up in it I'll tell you all about it.' And he began to tell the outline of the strange story behind the *Ascania*'s cargo, a tale which was filled out in more detail in the newspapers of the next few days.

In Pittsburgh there lived a wealthy American industrialist named Robert G. Chesterfield. He owned a great steel foundry connected with the motor industry, and he had built up the entire business himself since starting work as a lad of fourteen in a general smithy. He was now worth a vast amount of money, one and a quarter million dollars of which he had decided to present to Britain.

Robert G. Chesterfield had a particular reason for making this gift. He had himself been born in England, and his parents had lived in Sheffield, where his father was a foundry worker. One day when he was only three years old, part of a wall had collapsed in the wind while he was playing on the pavement, and he had been seriously injured. That he survived at all was due to the extraordinary patience and skill of a local surgeon, who had brought him safely through the first critical days and had gradually restored him to a state in which he could walk and run and play again, even though his spine was permanently bent just below his shoulder blades.

In those days there was no National Health Service, and Robert's father could not afford to pay very much for the doctor's services. In fact he did not pay anything, for Dr Hemming refused to take any payment at all, although he was by no means a rich doctor.

Two years later times were bad in the Yorkshire steel mills and Robert's father decided to emigrate to the United States, where industry was expanding rapidly. He worked his passage across as a stoker, whilst his wife and Robert travelled steerage on the same cargo ship. The voyage took a fortnight, but the family eventually reached Pittsburgh, where the father easily found work. When he died of consumption nine years later it was left to Robert to support his mother. Forty years later Robert G. Chesterfield was a millionaire industrialist.

Now that he was a wealthy man Chesterfield wanted to do something for the Sheffield doctor of whose kindness his mother had often told him, although he himself could remember nothing of England and had only the dimmest recollection of his voyage to America. But since Dr Hemming had long been dead, Chesterfield decided to present more than a million dollars to Britain to build and equip a hospital for crippled children. He expressly wished it to be called the Hemming Memorial Hospital.

Robert G. Chesterfield, however, was a bit of a crank, as so many great and successful business men are. He knew that it would be some time before the hospital could be built, and he was worried that the value of either American dollars or English pounds might fall – as both of them had done in the past few years. So instead of paying the money over into a bank account in England, or holding it in America, he purchased old gold coins and plate from every source he could hear of, and had it melted down in his own foundry. A casting mould bearing a monogram of his initials was made, and ingots were cast as fast as the gold could be obtained. When, after two years, the whole amount had been got together, Chesterfield's works strong-room contained one hundred and four gold ingots, each weighing about twenty pounds and worth some four thousand pounds apiece.

When all was ready he cabled the Ministry of Health in London announcing his gift, and a few days later the ingots were crated up in boxes of eight and shipped aboard the *Ascania* in New York. The consignment was safely stowed in the ship's strong-room, and in due time the *Ascania* sailed for Southampton.

For safety, both the Bank of England and Robert G. Chesterfield himself had agreed from the start that the gift was not to be announced publicly until the gold was safely delivered, but it was obvious to the bank that thousands of people in Pittsburgh, in the New York docks and among the crew of the *Ascania* would certainly know that the gold was on the move. So they drew up a careful plan for transferring the gold from Southampton to London, and submitted the scheme to Scotland Yard for their approval. That was how Michael's father knew about it, and he knew too that Sergeant Denby was to accompany the gold on its journey from Southampton. In fact he himself had suggested Denby for the job.

'I could have sworn it was foolproof,' he repeated, glancing out of the back window to see if there was any sign of the police cars approaching. 'But I was wrong. Well, there's nothing for it but to see what we can pick up in the way of clues at the scene of the robbery. I'm not too hopeful, but at least we know one good thing. Such a large amount of gold will take some disposing of. We ought to be able to spot the stuff when it starts finding its way into the trade. There's nearly a ton of it. They'll never get it out of the country without being caught.'

'In any case it would be insured,' said Denby.

'You're wrong there. It wasn't. The old boy was a crank about insurance too. He wouldn't even allow the bank to "waste good brass on a lot of hi-jacking underwriters". That's what he said, apparently.'

'You mean that if it's lost it's just gone, and there'll be no hospital?' asked Michael quietly.

'I'm afraid so, Michael.' Mr Branxome drummed impatiently on the steering wheel with his fingers. 'What would your Mr Gregson have to say about that?'

'I don't know, Daddy,' Michael replied. 'But I know you'll have to get the gold back again, that's all.'

When the first faint light of midsummer began to drive back the dark over the Hampshire countryside the railway line a mile and a half on the up side of Micheldever station was a scene of great activity. Police photographers were taking flashlight photographs of the scene of the robbery, and while the ground was being examined for any possible clues Chief-superintendent Branxome and Sergeant Denby were giving all the information they could to the county police inspector.

Denby confirmed that the arrangements at Southampton had all gone according to plan. The *Ascania* had docked there, and as soon as the passengers and luggage were disembarked the ship's strong-room was opened up and the cases of gold were checked as they came ashore and checked again as they were loaded into the railway van. It had been decided that the safest means of bringing the gold to London was by a special parcels van attached to the rear of the *Ascania* boat train which would run to London without a stop. This van was carefully guarded in the docks until the train was actually under way, and Sergeant Denby was posted inside the van to accompany the gold from Southampton to Waterloo.

With Denby's story and what the police had discovered by telephone from the railway terminus in London, the broad outline of events was becoming clear. The train had been making good time until up beyond Micheldever station, when the signal for the following section was found to be set at danger. There was nothing particularly unusual about such an event, and the driver halted the train just short of the signal. He blew on his whistle, and waited. Denby got up and looked through the barred windows on either side of the van, but he saw nothing suspicious. After a couple of minutes or so the signal arm was swung up, the green light showed, and the train continued on its journey. It was not until its arrival at Waterloo that the loss of the van at the rear was discovered by the train crew, and by that time the police were already investigating the empty van where it stood forlornly on the up line, its broken doors hanging open and the red lights still shining at the rear.

Denby himself had hardly realised that the train was rumbling off up the line without him when he heard a noise, and looking through the bars he dimly made out the figures of several men scrambling over the fence from the direction of the trees. The doors were padlocked on the outside and he quickly slipped home the bolts on his side too, but it seemed hardly a matter of seconds before the doors burst open under the levering force of heavy crowbars. Denby remembered a confused scuffle in the dark as he tried to hold the men off, but they got him by the legs and dragged him out. A pad was held over his face, and he remembered nothing more until he recovered consciousness lying among the trees with his hands tied behind him and the scarf over his mouth, as he had already reported.

One of the first inquiries made by the police was at the signal box up the line. The signalman swore that he had not touched the signal lever until after the boat train had passed his box, when he set it to danger until the following section rang through to confirm that they had accepted the train. The whole road was set for clear when the train was passed into his own section, but he did not see the train stop, because his box was more than a mile up the line and round a slight bend. He remembered hearing the whistle blown, but, as the train came through shortly afterwards, he thought nothing of it. Besides, a down train had passed only a few minutes earlier and it might have been blowing for the down signal at Micheldever, he pointed out.

At first the police received his tale with cautious doubt, but it was very soon confirmed, for some three hundred yards up from the signal post the wire which operated that particular signal was found to be cut. This would automatically drop the signal arm to danger, and halt the train, after which it would only be necessary to haul on the wire to pull the arm up to allow the train to proceed after it had been halted for the necessary time. Afterwards the signal had been dropped back to danger and left there, and, when the signal-man had moved his lever, it had not in fact been connected to the signal arm at all.

How the van had actually been uncoupled could not be known for certain, but it was at least possible to guess. Somebody must actually have disconnected the chain-shackles. Whoever unfastened the couplings while the train was stationary must have darted in as soon as it drew up, done his work, and either remained standing between the van and the rear coach or lain down beneath one of them to avoid detection. But however he had done the job he had done it well, for he had not forgotten to turn the tap to close off the vacuum brake where he disconnected the flexible pressure pipe between the last coach and the van. If this had not been done the vacuum of the brake system would have been broken and the train would not have been able to move ahead when given the green signal again. The whole job was carefully planned and cleverly carried out.

At last the police photographers finished taking their flashlight records of the scene, and a light tank engine which had been sent up from Winchester and had been waiting patiently at a respectful distance puffed slowly up, coupled on to the van and moved off sedately towards Micheldever to shunt it into a siding and clear the line again for normal working.

Michael watched it as it disappeared into the distance, half hidden by the rolling cloud of its own steam and smoke.

Mr Branxome came up behind and laid a hand on his shoulder. 'We can go now, Michael. There's nothing else we can do here. The experts have got all the information they can, and it doesn't amount to a great deal. No usable finger prints on the railway-van. Nothing left lying about. It's one of the neatest robberies I've ever seen.'

'So, apart from the signal wire being cut, they haven't found a thing.' Michael was still staring at where the van was running out of sight as the engine hauled it towards the country station.

'No. Except for Denby's shoes and socks. He discovered them himself, lying among the trees. I'm glad he got them back, aren't you?' He sensed Michael's disappointment and was trying to cheer him up.

'Oh yes,' replied Michael rather absently. 'Yes, Sergeant Denby must be pleased. But . . . well, I would rather it had been the gold that had turned up. What do you think they're going to say to Mr Chesterfield?'

'I suppose they'll just have to tell him,' replied his father. 'I'm afraid he may not take it very well.'

'Still, it wasn't really your fault that it happened,' said Michael doubtfully. 'All the same it makes us look rather stupid in England, doesn't it? And I don't like that.'

The chief-superintendent took Michael by the arm. 'Come on,' he said gently. 'You're tired, and no wonder.'

They set off together along the track to where their car stood beside the others at the edge of a field of clover. Even before they had bumped as far as the gate on to the main road Michael was fast asleep.

2. Message from Paris

It was the beginning of the holidays. Jill had just come home from an afternoon of tidying up at school, and Peter, her elder brother, had already been home for a couple of days from boarding school. Michael the youngest, still had another day to go before his term ended, but he had not yet arrived home. Peter and Jill were with their mother in the living-room, and Peter had raised the question of what they were going to do in the holidays. Usually their parents had planned things far ahead, but this time nothing seemed to have been fixed. The bullion robbery had cut across any plans which might have been made.

Jill liked school, because there people behaved naturally, but she always looked forward to the holidays when the family could all go away together and leave London far behind. Particularly if they went on the *Dabchick* and moored at the little country villages where the people were so very different from townsfolk, so much easier to get on with and so much more friendly. In the summer there was swimming, too, and Jill loved the water. She was a strong swimmer, had won the quarter-mile free style cup at school, and could dive well too, though her style was not good enough for her to come higher than fourth in the finals.

Jill got on well with her brothers, although in some ways they were both so different from herself. She sometimes found Peter a little quiet and serious, but she was glad that he was not like the brothers of some of her school friends who seemed to despise girls just because they were girls, and who could do nothing but talk about football and the insides of motor-cars. She was good friends with Michael too, and she shared his love for adventure even if she was not so anxious as he was to nose about in ditches and creeks and odd corners.

Jill was devoted to her father. Even before he spoke she could always tell when he was worried or when things were going well. At the moment, however, she was very puzzled, for although she had had a feeling for the last two or three days that her father was less worried than he had been before, he had said nothing to make her certain that a clue had been found. In fact he had been unusually silent and secretive.

Because Jill knew how particularly her father had taken to heart the loss of the Chesterfield gold, she was more concerned that he should solve the mystery than that they should all be able to go away for a holiday. Peter, however, was clearly disappointed, and rather hurt that family plans should have to be pushed into the background. Michael had taken the news badly too, and a week earlier there had been a bit of a scene about it.

Now that Peter had raised the subject again, Jill hoped that they could at least get the discussion over before Michael came in. The holidays were here at last, and she did not want them to start with everyone moody and upset. To her the holiday plans really were of no importance at all compared with her father's success in finding what had become of the gold.

Peter was staring rather gloomily out of the window. 'As for the holidays,' he said, 'I suppose it can't be helped. Of course it's a pity, because when Dad came down to see the school play he said we might perhaps be able to go somewhere abroad. It would have been fun, I know. Still, if Dad's really got to be in London all the time we can probably go on the river at the week-ends.'

'Hear, hear,' Jill said, trying to ease the atmosphere. 'We can manage perfectly well without going away at all, can't we? I know we had all wanted to go somewhere exciting if we could, but we can find plenty to do at home.'

'You two and Michael could go on the *Dabchick* by yourselves,' suggested their mother with a curious, secretive smile.

'Yes, of course we could,' Jill said quickly. 'We could go and explore right upstream farther than we have ever been.'

'I think she would get under the low bridge at Oxford,' Peter said, not very enthusiastically. 'If so, I suppose we could run right up to Lechdale. That would be better than nothing.'

'It would be grand,' Jill said. Then her enthusiasm seemed to fade a little. 'Still, that would mean leaving you behind, Mummy, if you were going to look after Daddy.' Suddenly she had an idea. 'Look, why don't you leave me to look after Daddy, and you three go away? Or better still, Peter and Michael and I can stay here and you can go up to see Aunt Mary in Edinburgh. You've been intending to for months, you know that.'

'Yes,' said Peter. 'If we can't all go away together, there's no reason why you should stay at home.'

'It's very sweet of you both, and perhaps I might go and see your aunt for a week or two. But if I were you I shouldn't worry too much about the holidays. Something might turn up which you hadn't even thought of.'

Michael was late home from school and he had only just

come in when Mr Branxome arrived back from the Yard. From the very way in which he strode into the room Jill sensed at once that he had had good news. She ran over and took his arm.

'Have they found the lorry, Dad?' she asked excitedly.

Her father laughed. 'We don't want the lorry now. We've got the gold – or some of it.' He flung down his case and dropped into the armchair by the window.

'What! Tell us, Daddy, quick,' exclaimed Michael.

'When was it found?' asked Jill.

'And where?' added Peter. 'Come on, Dad, tell us.'

Only their mother did not join in the general surprise. It seemed as though she had not heard.

Mr Branxome sank into his chair while they gathered round.

'When? Three days ago. Where? In Paris.' He waited with a tantalizing smile.

'How much has been found?' Michael wanted details.

'Only three bars, but we had a photograph flown over from the Sûreté. They're Chesterfield's right enough, with his monogram cast in the face. Now if you'll all give me the chance I'll tell you something else. I've got to go over to Paris tomorrow and probably I shall be flying to and fro between here and there for the next few weeks while we follow the scent with the French police. Your mother is going up next Friday to visit her sister in Scotland.' He stopped. 'That's all, isn't it?' He looked quickly at their mother. 'I don't think I've forgotten anything, have I?'

Michael thought he detected a quick wink exchanged by his parents before his mother replied. 'I can't think of anything else, unless – oh yes, I remember. There was that man you were going to speak to.'

'What man?' Their father looked puzzled.

'Something about Henley,' their mother went on with a quick sideways glance at the children. 'Or was it Dover?'

'Ah yes, I remember. You mean about Sergeant Tillman. Yes, that's all fixed. He's started.'

'Who is Sergeant Tillman?' Jill was unable to contain her curiosity any longer.

'Oh, he's just a fellow in the Thames Division,' replied her father as though he hardly knew.

'Is he going to France to help you?' Michael asked.

'With me? No. He's going to help three other people. I can tell you their names if you're interested.'

'Who are they, Daddy?' Michael was really curious.

'They're Peter Branxome, Jill Branxome and Michael Branxome,' said his father with a laugh.

'Daddy! Are we going to Paris too?' Jill asked.

'Sergeant Tillman left Henley yesterday morning on the *Dabchick*. By now he should be somewhere around Sheerness. Tomorrow he'll run her to Dover and the following morning if it's reasonably good weather you three and Tillman will put out from Dover and start for France, and Paris.'

'How super!' Michael exclaimed hopping from one foot to the other. 'I've always wanted to go to Paris.'

'It sounds lovely,' Peter agreed. 'But I thought you said we wouldn't be able to go away.' He turned to his mother as he spoke.

'I said so? It was you who said so, Peter, not me.'

'And you mean to say you knew this all the time?' Jill pointed accusingly at her mother. 'Why didn't you tell us?'

'You never asked me.' They all laughed, and for a minute or two there was excitement all round. Then Mr Branxome outlined the arrangement.

'You'll aim for Boulogne, I should imagine. Tillman is a very reliable man and he was petty officer on an M.T.B. in the coastal forces during the war. He knows the Channel like the back of his hand. Once you're over he is to come back to London and you can carry on. He says you just take a calm day and run right down about half a mile off shore till you get to the mouth of the Seine at Le Havre.'

'I hope you're remembering all this, Peter,' said Jill.

'Tillman has charts and a good compass aboard,' Mr Branxome continued. 'He'll give you all the details. He says you can't have any trouble down that part. There are no banks or anything to worry about apparently, and when you're at the Seine you just run right up till you get to Paris. He reckons it will take you a week from Boulogne even if you're not held up by bad weather. That's why I thought he had better start right away and save two or three days by getting the *Dabchick* as far as Dover for you.'

'That's a good idea, Dad,' Peter agreed.

'It's a pity Mummy has to miss going to Paris,' said Jill.

'I'm not missing it,' her mother reassured her. 'When you're there I shall probably fly straight out from Edinburgh.'

'How exciting,' Michael almost shouted. 'So we'll all be there at once.'

'That's the idea,' Mr Branxome said. 'We can combine business and pleasure. It's even possible that by the time you get there we shall have traced the bullion thieves.'

'When did you decide all this?' Peter asked.

'As soon as I heard the gold was beginning to turn up in Paris. It was all your mother's idea, except for getting Tillman to start ahead to Dover – that was mine.'

'Well, I still think it was the limit, keeping it secret like that,' said Jill with a smile. 'But we'll forgive you, and we'll get to Paris all right, you see if we don't.'

'Passports!' said Michael suddenly.

'Don't worry. The forms are in my bag for each of you to sign, and the passports will be ready to be picked up down in Petty France tomorrow.'

'Petty France? Where on earth is that?' asked Jill.

'Down by St. James's Park. It's the name of the street where the Passport Office is.'

'What's the opposite of "Petty", Daddy?' giggled Michael.

'"Grand", I suppose. Petty was "Petit" once no doubt.'

'Then we're off to Grand France – isn't that grand?'

Soon it was supper time, and afterwards Jill and her mother went through to the larder to put out a few stores to take down to the boat at Dover and add to the supplies already on board, though most of the stores were to be bought in France as they went along. Meanwhile, Peter and his father were looking at a map of the Continent, and making arrangements about money and all the odds and ends that might be necessary on board. Michael was given the job of getting some more bedding sorted out and after that he was to go to bed. Rather reluctantly he went up to his room, undressed, and got into bed.

'I hope you don't mind my sending Tillman over with you, Peter,' his father said. 'You could have run over without him, I know, but there are only three of you and you might run into bad visibility or something. I thought it would be better.'

'I suppose you're right,' Peter agreed hesitantly. 'All the same, it's a pity we can't do everything for ourselves. I'm sure Sergeant Tillman is very pleasant and all that, but it's not quite the same as when we're alone.'

'H'm. I can see that,' said his father.

There was silence for a moment before Peter spoke. 'Look, Dad,' he said finally, 'wouldn't it be all right if we went on our own, right from Dover? After all, we've been on the sea before. Supposing I promise you not to put out from Dover unless the sea is reasonably calm and the shipping forecast is favourable, would that be all right?'

His father considered. 'Well, I suppose so. The engine has had a complete overhaul and is perfectly sound, so there's no reason why you should have any trouble.'

'Besides,' added Peter, 'it's quite a busy crossing. If we did get stuck we would be able to get help before long, I'm sure. And we really will be sensible and not try to cross unless it is absolutely suitable.'

'H'm. Yes, perhaps it might be all right. There's a good compass aboard at the moment, and I'll have a message sent to Tillman to ask him to leave it aboard with the charts. But don't take any risks.'

'Don't worry, Dad, I won't. And thanks for letting us go on our own. I think the others will be pleased too.'

Michael called to his father from upstairs, and Mr Branxome left Peter looking up the tidal streams in the nautical tables while he went up.

Michael was the youngest of the family, and from as far back as he could remember he had never wanted to become anything but an officer in the C.I.D., like his father. It would be exciting, and Michael liked things that were difficult and exciting at the same time, particularly if they involved a bit of nosing about. He liked the kind of lessons at school where you had to find out about things for yourself, but even more he loved being aboard the *Dabchick* when the holidays came round, because wherever they decided to go there were always all sorts of strange things to be investigated, and there was plenty of adventure too. It might be racing the steamers into the locks, or just nosing the dinghy into the little streams and backwaters along the banks, or rowing hard up the side of a weir race to turn at the last moment into the surging rush of water and be twisted round and down into the pool like a cork – there was always plenty to occupy Michael.

If anybody lost anything it was always Michael who found it. In fact he was always finding things unexpectedly. Once he found a half-crown amongst the stones near the edge of the river, and he often returned from exploring in the dinghy with strange booty – a ball, a fender lost overboard from another boat, water-mussel shells, or an old clay pipe. And besides this he was becoming quite a crafty fisherman. More than once he had gone out in the dinghy and silently angled an eel from between the piles of an old mill on nights when, as he explained, it was too dark to see the notice 'Private Fishing'.

To go to Paris in the *Dabchick* was an idea so exciting that he was impatient to be away. He didn't care how much the boat would roll – in fact he liked it. He wanted only to be off on a journey which would provide all sorts of new adventures. Besides, he wanted if possible to get to Paris before his father and the French police had finally solved the mystery of the Chesterfield gold. He didn't want to miss the finish, particularly after he had been in at the beginning that night down beside the railway line in Hampshire.

'There's something I don't understand, Daddy,' said Michael at once as his father came into his bedroom. 'You say that the gold is now turning up in Paris, but three weeks ago you said that if there was one thing absolutely certain it was that nobody could get the bars out of the country without being caught.'

Mr Branxome sat down on the bed and nodded. 'You're right, and down at the Yard we're just as puzzled as you are. The day after we were at Micheldever the most elaborate check was started at every port in the country, and it is still imposed. If you go on a channel boat your luggage is searched from end to end. There's not a package goes into the London docks or any other docks without its source and contents being thoroughly checked.'

'What about planes?'

'They're all watched just as thoroughly, and even if some small private plane left this country and landed in France it would be traced.'

'Unless it landed in some out-of-the-way field,' suggested Michael.

'No. Radar stations can check every aircraft leaving or entering, and they do so as a matter of course. There has not been a single flight except for routine passenger and transport planes, and a few charter aircraft which have flown from airports and landed at airports.'

Michael thought hard for a moment. 'How about smuggling it through by the train ferry?'

His father shook his head. 'No. That route has been checked high and low.'

'And private cars?'

'The same. The customs men have practically crawled down the fillers of the petrol tanks. The thing is absolutely baffling.'

Michael considered again. 'I know how I would take it

across, Daddy,' he exclaimed excitedly. 'I would take it in a yacht – like the *Dabchick*. Nobody would think of stopping a yacht.'

Mr Branxome laughed. 'You haven't much of an opinion of us, have you? Right from the beginning we thought of that one, and there's not a sailing-boat or fishing-boat or yacht or anything puts out from Britain but the coastguards go through it from stem to stern.'

Michael was disappointed. 'Even the bilge?' he suggested hopefully.

'Even the bilge. No, the gold is getting across to Paris, but it's not leaving the country by boat or by plane. I'm certain of that. The question is, how else could it go? Have you any other ideas?'

'Submarine,' suggested Michael at once.

'There aren't any private submarines, fortunately.'

Michael had to think again. 'Well, if I were a crook I might melt down the gold and beat it out into mudguards and things, fix them on a car and paint them, and drive the car across right under the noses of the customs people,' he said triumphantly.

'That's not a bad idea,' said his father thoughtfully. 'Not a bad idea at all. You know, Michael, you would make a good crook, and an even better detective. The only snag in this case is that the gold has not been melted down. It has turned up in the same big twenty-pound bars it was in before.'

'Where were they found?'

'It hasn't been made public, but if you won't tell anybody –'

'Of course not, Daddy. I never do, you know that.'

'Yes, I know. Well, the French police report says that a constable challenged a man somewhere in the Latin Quarter about nine o'clock in the morning. The fellow was carrying a suitcase, and although it was not very large it was obviously heavy, and the policeman thought the man was very likely a burglar. When challenged he ran off, but in the next street he was tackled by a passer-by who heard the police whistle and saw him running. In the scuffle he dropped the case and disappeared into the crowds in the Metro – that's the Paris underground – and escaped. The case contained three of our bullion bars and nothing else.'

'I suppose the Latin Quarter is a sort of haunt of crooks?'

'In a way, but it isn't called that because of all the Italians who live there. It was once the area of the university and of all the scholars and professors, and Latin was spoken there as the language of the learned men.'

'I say, how queer. If we go to the Latin Quarter I suppose we shall have to talk Latin too. Shopping will be fun. I can just imagine Jill marching into the grocer's and asking for *panis* and *pisces* and – what would potatoes be? They didn't have them in the days of the Romans. Nor sausages. At least I've never come across them in the Latin Prose we do at school, though that's mostly about the emperor sending out messengers and the legionaries attacking the town with tortoises and the citizens defending themselves with catapults.'

His father laughed. 'No, I'm afraid they don't speak Latin there any longer. You'll just have to ask for *pommes de terre* and *saucissons.*'

Two days later a taxi was making its way from Dover Marine station along the promenade and past the memorial commemorating Captain Webb's first successful cross-Channel swim. The Channel itself was hidden from view by the great arms of the harbour walls except where a gap in the Western Arm revealed the rough heaving of a nasty sea beyond. Just occasionally as the waves struck the corners of the opening a cloud of spray exploded upwards, flung so high in the air that it rose right up above the arm itself. Overhead the clouds were racing across the top of the cliffs to disappear inland.

Jill was looking out of the window of the taxi. She did not say anything but Peter knew the thoughts in her mind.

'No,' he said, following the direction of her gaze. 'It doesn't look too good just at the moment.'

'Oh, I don't know,' said Michael hopefully. 'It may not be half as bad as it looks. It would be much more fun if it was not too calm.'

'No,' said Peter definitely. 'We're not going across in this weather.'

They followed the line of cars driving down to the Eastern Dock loaded with luggage for continental holidays, but at the approach to the ferry terminal their way branched to the left to continue alone along the narrow road at the foot of the cliffs.

'Submarine basin, you said, sir?' the taximan asked.

'That's right.'

'It's away round the end there, sir.' And he drove on behind naval workshops and past great heaps of scrap, skirting the edge of the harbour until their route lay along the top of the Eastern Arm itself and past the tanker berths.

Some way ahead lay a handsome ship with a maze of wireless aerials. Her hull was hidden from view below the wall but her bridge was showing and steam was rising gently from her tall red funnel.

'She's got steam up,' said the taxi-driver with a nod towards the vessel. 'That's a bad sign.'

'Why is it a bad sign?' Michael asked.

'She's a tug –'

'What! A tug that size?'

'Yes, she's an ocean-going tug. She's kept stationed here by Lloyd's in case any ships run into trouble in the Straits. When she has steam up it's a sign that she's ready to run out, and that means there's dirty weather about and she knows it.'

The taxi pulled up where a side arm ran off to the right towards a group of heavily roofed pens in which some small naval craft were parked like cars in garages. 'This is it, sir,' the driver said, and they climbed out into a wind that nearly blew them off the quay.

Down at the foot of the high wall on the landward side of the short arm the *Dabchick* lay alone, moored up to the ladder on slack ropes where Sergeant Tillman had left her to rise and fall with the tide. Peter paid the taxi, and they assembled their luggage at the top of the ladder.

'I'll go down and fling up a line,' Peter said. 'Then you can let the things down to me and follow.' He lowered himself over the edge of the quay and descended cautiously towards the boat.

'Mind how you come down,' he shouted up as he flung a light line up to the quayside. 'The steps are slippery. Hold on tight.'

On board everything was shipshape and a note from Sergeant Tillman lay on the table of the forward cabin along with a number of charts.

Sir, [it ran] the tank is full and everything is ready. Weather looks bad, but might clear away. When leaving, take the left-hand entrance, as the other is blocked by a ship sunk 1914–18. At Le Havre there is a canal by-passing the estuary up to Tancarville. You should take the canal, as the estuary can be tricky on a bad tide. The *Dabchick* is a good craft and I had a pleasant run in her, though she is a bit slow against a tide. – Yours truly, D. TILLMAN.

Peter read out the message and glanced at the charts. 'There's no hope today,' he declared, rather to Jill's relief.

'Oh, I don't see why not,' urged Michael. 'Couldn't we just run out of the harbour and see what it's like?'

Peter looked at him disapprovingly. 'No, Michael. If you care to run up the ladder again and look across to the signal station at the entrance you will see a triangular object suspended from the mast. That's a South Cone. I saw it as we drove along the jetty.'

'Well?'

'I suppose you know what a South Cone is.' Peter himself did, because he had seen a diagram of it only the night before, when browsing through the *Nautical Almanac*. 'It means a gale from the South-East, round through South to North-

West, and the point of the triangle is downwards. When the point is upwards it's a North Cone, and the gale is from the other half of the compass. And if you want to know, a gale is a wind of force eight or higher on the Beaufort scale.'

'Thanks,' said Michael. 'I thought I had finished lessons for a few weeks with term ending yesterday.'

'Let's unpack,' said Jill quickly. 'Then we can go up on the wall and have a look round. And of course I'll need to do something about lunch.'

They soon had their things stowed away, and as there were only three of them to sleep in the boat, Peter and Michael shared the larger stern cabin which really belonged to their parents, and Jill was installed alone in the forward cabin, usually shared by the three of them, although Peter's legs were already becoming too long for the bunks. The stores were quickly packed away in the galley, and soon they were ready to climb up the ladder again to the top of the wall.

Up above, the wind was still driving over the top, and Jill's hair streamed in the wind. Michael gazed out across the harbour towards the signal station.

'Which is the cone you were talking about, Peter?'

'On the mast. Can't you see it?'

'No.'

Peter turned to look too. 'It must have been taken down,' he said.

Michael giggled. 'I think you imagined it.'

'How could I imagine a South Cone? It's gone, right enough, and that's a good sign. It means either that the gale has gone for good, or that there is a lull of not less than twelve hours expected.'

'There's still an awful wind,' Jill pointed out.

'Yes. We can't expect it to die out in five minutes. It may take days.'

'Oh, not days, surely,' Michael objected. 'Hours perhaps, but not days. It might be quite calm by tea-time.'

Peter shook his head. 'It will take a while for this sea to

die down even if the wind does drop. Still, there's no use talking about it. We shall just have to wait and see. The trouble with English weather is that you can never tell what it's going to do.' Secretly he was beginning to wish that he had not persuaded his father to let them cross to France alone. Sergeant Tillman might have been able to read the sky and tell him just which way the weather was developing.

3. Tea and the Compass

Doing nothing can be a tiring business and by bedtime that night the crew of the *Dabchick* were bored and sleepy. Michael and Jill turned in soon after nine but Peter climbed up the ladder once more and went up the steps to the rampart-like walk on the outer side of the Eastern Arm. Down below, the heavy rollers were sweeping past to thunder against the chalk at the foot of the cliffs and the water hissed and seethed defiantly. The wind, however, had dropped considerably.

Out at sea Peter could make out the forms of four cargo ships running out towards the Atlantic. Two were well out from the land but the others were close inshore. He stared at them, trying to make out whether they were pitching at all, but they seemed to glide smoothly on their way without so much as noticing the sea. Only the occasional sheet of spray flung up at their bows showed that the waves were bigger than they appeared from a distance.

To Michael the idea of running the *Dabchick* to France was just an exciting adventure. Probably if he had been Peter's age he would still have thought of it in much the same way. But Peter was by nature very different. It was not that he lacked courage; on the contrary, he could be relied upon to act quickly and calmly in any emergency, and it was perhaps this particular part of his character which had persuaded his father to leave the voyage in his hands without the aid of Sergeant Tillman.

Peter was a person who took his duties and responsibilities very seriously – too seriously, some of his school friends thought, and once his headmaster had written on his report, 'A valuable member of the school. Always conscientious, helpful and reliable – but could he laugh at himself, just once?' Not that Peter minded the remark. He dismissed it as one of the things which a headmaster liked to say.

He was not brilliant – Michael had the greatest share of the brains as well as of natural bubbling gaiety – but Peter did well at school in both work and in sports through sheer determination and careful, thorough effort. Michael thought him over-cautious, but he was wrong. Peter's decision not to run out of Dover in bad weather was not due either to lack of courage or to being too careful, but rather to his sense of responsibility and his concern for others.

Peter knew that he was responsible for the safety of his younger brother and sister, and he did not regard this responsibility with pride, but took it as a natural duty. He knew too that Jill disliked the sea when it was at all rough, and he would never subject her or anybody else to anything which she would not wish for herself. If he had been alone he would have run the *Dabchick* across as soon as the storm had passed its peak, for he knew that she was a fine and seaworthy craft, but with Jill and Michael aboard he would not put out unless he could be sure of an easy voyage.

His last glance before returning on board was towards the signal mast, but there was no cone showing and a return of the gale was evidently not expected. Back on board he pored over the charts again and eventually went to his cabin and quietly got into bed.

There's no better place for a good sound sleep than on board a small boat in a harbour, and in the submarine basin at Dover the *Dabchick*'s crew were asleep as soon as they were in bed. Though well sheltered from the seas driving into the main harbour, the water by the pens rose and fell ever so gently as the surge came through the narrow entrance, and the *Dabchick* rocked sweetly in her corner with a gentle graceful motion that kept her crew deep in the ocean of dreams.

When Peter at last awoke and looked at his watch he jumped out of his bunk so suddenly that Michael sat up with a jerk.

'What is it, Peter?'

'It's just on five to seven. I must get the forecast again.' Without even waiting to put on his socks he hurried through, and up the companion ladder to the deck. Tumbling into the wheelhouse he turned on the wireless. By the time the valves had warmed and the sound was coming through, the announcer was just finishing the general weather forecast with its doubts about 'probably mainly fair and cloudy with occasional rain and bright intervals'. Then with a rustle of paper came the shipping forecast for the period up to noon.

'Iceland, Faroes, Bailey, Hebrides, Rockall, Malin . . .' Still blowing a gale, Peter noted. 'Irish Sea, Shannon, Fastnet, Lundy, fresh to strong west to south westerly winds, moderating. Visibility good.' And Sole, Finisterre and Biscay were the same but southerly. Plymouth, Portland and Wight had only moderate winds, south to south-east.

'Dover, Thames. Light to moderate south-easterly winds, visibility good.'

Michael joined Peter in the wheelhouse. 'What's the fore-cast, Peter?'

Peter held up his hand and the voice droned on through Humber and Heligoland, Tyne, Forth and Cromarty to Dogger and Forties. As the forecast came to an end he clicked off the switch.

'It looks pretty good,' he said. 'The farther down our way the calmer. Light to moderate is good enough for us. We'll get dressed quickly and get moving.'

'Hooray!' Michael ran excitedly along the catwalk to disappear below and wake Jill.

It was only a matter of minutes before the *Dabchick* was drawing away from the wall. Michael was at the wheel whilst Peter consulted the *Almanac* for the rate and direction of tide.

'About one hour since high tide,' he muttered to himself. 'That means the tide is now running east at a couple of knots. The next hour it's only running at about one knot and the same for the third hour; but the fourth hour it should be slipping a knot or so to the west.' He added the figures. 'If it takes us four hours, that's a total drift to the east of three miles, near enough, so we make our bearing for three miles west of Boulogne and we should be dead on the mark.' He laid a ruler across the chart from Dover to a point beyond the Cap d'Alprech, west of Boulogne. 'That's the line,' he said out loud, and noting the bearing he set the compass.

Michael ran through the exit of the basin into the main harbour and headed for the left-hand entrance as Sergeant Tillman's note had told them to, but he was only a third of the way across the main harbour when a launch appeared running up fast from the direction of the railway quay. He slackened speed as the boat drew level and a customs officer standing in the well signalled to him to stop. Peter opened the door of the wheelhouse and leant out.

'Where are you for?' the officer asked as his boat drew in until the two craft were nearly touching.

'Paris,' Peter answered.

'Draw over to the jetty, please. Follow us.'

The craft drew away again, turned a sweep and headed slowly up the harbour with the *Dabchick* following a short way astern. Jill's head appeared through the hatch.

'What is it, Peter?' she asked.

'Customs,' he told her as he stood at the rail. 'Can you come up? I'll need your help to tie up.'

Right at the far end of the harbour the leading boat drew in to the wall beside the Wellington Dock, and Michael eased off to bring the *Dabchick* up astern of her but the officer signalled him to come alongside.

'Sorry to delay you,' he said pleasantly as his watermen took the lines which Jill and Peter threw across the boat. 'I shall not keep you long.' He stepped aboard and Peter followed him to the hatchway, with Jill and Michael behind.

The first thing was passports, and after glancing at them briefly the officer handed them back. 'I'm afraid I must look through the ship,' he said apologetically. 'We'll start here.' He pulled out the drawers below the bunks and explored under the towels and teacloths with his hands.

'Please lift the floor-traps.'

Michael bent down and pulled up the loose section of the floor while the others sat on Jill's bunk and lifted their legs out of the way.

'Thank you.' The officer knelt down, produced a flash-lamp from his pocket and shone the beam into one bilge compartment after another.

At the rear of the cabin some heavy blocks of pig-iron ballast were ranged along the bottom of the bilge, dirty and oily from the swilling of the water among them. The officer pulled out a pen-knife and scraped a little piece of the dull lead paint off each bar, then shone his lamp closely on the bare surface.

'Ah!' exclaimed Michael, 'I suppose you're looking for gold.'

The officer hesitated for a moment. 'Gold?' he said curiously.

'Yes,' Michael replied. 'You thought the ballast might be bullion bars painted over. Not at all a bad idea.'

Seeing the smiles of amusement on the faces of Jill and Peter the customs man stood up. 'What do you know about gold?' he asked, watching them closely.

'It's all right,' said Jill. 'We just happen to know all about the gold that was stolen from the *Ascania* boat train, because our father has something to do with it.'

'I was with him at the scene of the robbery,' added Michael proudly.

The officer gave a sarcastic grin. 'Sure you weren't driving the engine?'

'Quite sure,' replied Michael firmly. 'I was helping Daddy.'

'He was, really,' said Peter as the customs man shook his head.

The officer drew himself up and looked at them sternly. 'It's no use you trying to fool me that you stole the gold. And whoever said I was looking for gold, anyway?'

Michael burst out laughing. 'We never said we had stolen the gold,' he giggled. 'My Daddy is at Scotland Yard. He isn't a crook, he's in the C.I.D. And as for whether you're looking for the gold in our bilge – well, why else would you be chipping the paint off our ballast?'

'All right, all right, I am looking for gold, then,' said the officer rather huffily. He dropped back on his knees and stuck his head down below the floor. 'But I'm not swallowing that tale about you and your father and Scotland Yard.'

'You needn't if you don't want to,' said Peter. 'And if you want to search the whole boat you can. We'll put the floor boards back when you've finished.'

The search took nearly half an hour, and the crew followed the officer round, lifting mattresses, puffing up the pillows again after he had prodded them, opening and shutting drawers and replacing all the ropes and gear which he had pulled out of the after lockers. When at last he came to the end he straightened his back and put on his cap again.

'Sorry to have troubled you,' he said pleasantly enough. 'You can go on your way across now.'

'Thank you,' said Jill.

'I'm sure Daddy will be pleased when we tell him how well you searched the boat,' said Michael with a grin.

The officer paused on the companion-way as though he was going to reply, but he did not say anything. Instead he gave a little bray in imitation of a donkey and stepped aboard his launch.

The others followed on to the deck, the ropes were cast off, and Peter pushed out at the stern with his feet. Michael was at the wheel and he drew the *Dabchick* slowly out stern first until he had room to turn. Then as he swung round to head for the harbour entrance he waved to the officer.

'Goodbye, Admiral,' called the customs man. Then shaking his head he disappeared into the well of the launch.

Jill ran quickly below to finish her job of stuffing the cushions in among the crockery just in case there should be any rolling, and when she came up again the *Dabchick* was running out past the pier heads into the humpy swirl where the rebound from the shore met the tide as it swept past the entrance. She held on to the rail tightly as she made her way to the wheelhouse.

'Everything's safe below,' she said.

'Good.' Peter had taken over from Michael and was running the boat up to its compass bearing. 'A couple of hours and we shall see France,' he said. 'Four hours or less and we should be at Boulogne, but if the sea is reasonable we might as well cut off to the west a bit and start down the coast towards Le Havre.'

'Good show,' said Michael. 'All the same, I hope it won't be too calm. It's no fun on the sea if it's like the lake in Regent's Park.'

'It doesn't look as though it will be,' said Jill. 'There's quite a bit of movement as it is.'

'It may be better when we're clear of the coast,' Peter said. 'There's always a bit of a chop round bays and headlands. Out ahead it looks pretty good. No white horses at all.'

'Good,' said Jill, rather relieved. 'But even if the weather is good you're surely not going to try and go right to Le Havre without stopping, are you?'

'Well, we could, but what would the crew like?'

'Let's go on,' said Michael.

'Let's run across first and then see,' said Jill more cautiously.

'That's sensible,' Peter agreed. 'We'll make up for Boulogne first, and decide our plans when we get there.'

The sea was surprisingly gentle so soon after a gale, but when the wind had died away on the previous evening the powerful rollers had slowly begun to lose their fierceness and the force of the tide running through the Straits had got to work upon the waves, knocking them down and gradually transforming an angry sea into a docile and friendly piece of water. After the change of tide shortly before midnight there was little left but the slow heaving of a creased surface where recently the big seas had been curling and breaking. There was very little wind on the following morning, for it was still too early for the breeze to have got up, and so the *Dabchick* was making good time.

An hour out of Dover the English coastline had disappeared and they were surrounded on all sides by an expanse of water that faded away in the distance beneath the morning haze.

'I'm hungry,' admitted Jill. 'I'll go below and rake together some breakfast.'

'I'll help,' Michael said. 'Call down if you want us, Peter. . . .' And together they disappeared below.

Michael insisted on scrambled eggs. It was the only dish he could make, but he was as expert an egg scrambler as might have been found among all the great chefs of Soho. Whilst he prepared his mixture in a bowl and added just the right amount of salt and pepper and milk and butter Jill got out the plates and cutlery and put the kettle on to boil for the tea. Michael insisted that scrambled eggs could not be delayed once they had begun to cook in the pan, so he first helped Jill set out the rest of the breakfast on the chart table in the wheelhouse before he put his pan on the primus in the galley. As soon as he was ready to begin, Jill made the tea in the stainless steel teapot, put a cosy on it and carried it up to the wheelhouse. Michael stayed below to finish his masterpiece.

Peter and Jill had not long to wait before the hatch flew open again and Michael ran along the catwalk carefully balancing his pan.

'Quick,' he called. 'Quick. Serve it out, Jill, and we'll eat it right away.'

His efforts had certainly been successful, and the others complimented him on his cooking. 'It is good, isn't it?' he said proudly. 'I think scrambled eggs are usually so awful when you have them in a café. You know, all hard and running with water.'

'Hear, hear,' agreed Peter. 'But these are wonderful.'

'I shan't bother to clear away just now,' remarked Jill when they had all finished their breakfast. 'We shall have plenty of time to wash up later when I've heated up some water. It will be easier when we're over the other side.'

'We should see the coast before long,' said Peter, peering through the windshield. 'In fact I thought I caught just a glimpse of it a moment ago, but when you've been staring out into the bright haze all this time your eyes seem to go queer.'

Michael scanned the distance ahead. 'Yes,' he cried suddenly. 'There, look! I saw the line of the cliffs in the haze.'

Jill followed his finger. 'I think I see,' she said.

'I don't,' said Peter, 'but that doesn't mean the coastline isn't there.' He looked at his watch. 'We should only be about an hour and a half away from Boulogne by now. If you saw the cliffs they might be around the Cap d'Alprech. The chart shows them as pretty high.'

But the haze obstinately refused to lift and reveal the coast clearly, though a darker shadow behind it clearly indicated land. They had run for another half-hour before Jill pointed ahead on the starboard bow.

'Look! There, above the mist. Wireless masts.'

Peter saw them too and he looked at the chart. 'They're on the Cap,' he said. 'We must be within three or four miles. We've certainly made good time.'

'Peter,' said Michael in a strange voice. 'Are you sure your bearing is right?'

'Of course. Why?'

'Well . . .' Michael opened the door and leaned out to get an even clearer view. 'Those masts are exactly like the ones on the cliff above Dover.'

'Don't be silly,' scoffed Peter. He glanced again at the compass to make sure the needle was lying along the line which he had set.

'And another thing,' Michael persisted. 'You can see a long low mass just to the left of them. You know what that is? It's Dover Castle.'

'Nonsense,' objected the skipper.

'Look, Peter, look at the sun,' exclaimed Jill. 'When we left it was shining over on the left. Now it's on our right and slightly astern. We must have turned right round.'

There was no contradicting this evidence. Peter stared at the sun, then at the compass. 'I can't see how . . .'

Michael remembered the direction-finding dodge which he had learned in his scout troop at school. He quickly pulled the watch out of his pocket and placed it on the table with the hour hand pointing towards the sun. 'South is halfway between the hour hand and the twelve,' he said. 'That means we're running practically due North.'

'But we can't have turned round without noticing,' Peter began. 'Though we certainly seem to have done so,' he added.

Suddenly Michael laughed. 'Idiots that we are,' he exclaimed. He leaned over the chart table, lifted up the tea-

pot under its cosy, and drew it away. The compass needle
swung slowly round through nearly half a circle.

The others joined in his amusement. 'I never thought
about that,' said Jill.

'Nor did I,' admitted Peter. 'The moral is, if you must
drink tea in the wheelhouse don't use a steel pot.' He spun
the wheel over and turned the *Dabchick* back on her right
course.

Michael and Jill removed the knives and forks as well and
the tray too, and put them on the floor at the back of the
wheelhouse.

'I suppose we have wasted a lot of time over that,' Jill
said.

'A couple of hours probably,' Peter agreed. 'Still, it can't
be helped. We'll just have to carry on, but there'll be no
more tea till we get to Boulogne.'

By the time they had reached mid-Channel the haze
was still lying thick on the English coast but the French
side was clearing. Away to starboard Michael made out
a distant buoy and Peter identified it from the chart as
the mark for the upper end of the Varne Bank. Right down
beyond it a shape which he had taken to be a fishing-boat
was obviously the Varne Light Vessel. 'We're dead on
course now,' he said with satisfaction. 'That's the Cap
d'Alprech over to the right, and Gris Nez right round to the
left.'

'How long will it take us now?' asked Jill.

'A couple of hours, not more.'

'I think the sea seems to be coming up just a little,' she
said. Jill loved the sea, but she preferred it not to be rough,
even though she had never been actually sick.

Peter had noticed too that the wind was beginning to
freshen. 'I'll close the land over to port,' he said consider-
ately. He was anxious not to make the voyage unpleasant
in any respect, and there was the promise to his father as
well. 'If we run up for that church tower there at Audresselles we can then make up along the shore under the lee of

the cliffs.' He turned the wheel and headed the *Dabchick* farther north on the French coast.

Peter knew very well that the English Channel had a will of its own and did not listen to the bland voice of the weather forecast in order to decide how it was to behave. It could change its face in a surprisingly short time, and it had evidently decided to do so just on this particular morning. There was no doubt at all that the wind was freshening, coming in curious gusts like the puffs of the little cherubs in the corners of the maps drawn by sixteenth-century navigators.

Strange humpy seas were slapping at the *Dabchick*, and the swell of the old storm combined with the waves driven by the new wind from a different quarter to make a sea that was not dangerous but certainly unpleasant, if only because it was muddled and the waves came from every direction. Peter was alert for each of the bigger ones as they came, and at first he headed straight at them. But although the *Dabchick* rode them well the waves took all the way off her and a big one would stop her practically dead.

'I'll sidle them,' he muttered. 'We'll roll a good deal I'm afraid, but at least we shall not be stopped in our tracks.' And he approached each sea obliquely, rolling off the crest into the trough on the other side and then setting the ship on course again to make up another thirty or forty yards towards the coast before turning to sidle up the next slope.

'I say,' exclaimed Michael excitedly. 'This is super.'

Peter laughed shortly and glanced at Jill, who looked pale as she stared ahead at the waves. He put one arm on her shoulder for a brief moment. 'It won't be long,' he said quietly. 'I'm sorry I never thought about the teapot. We should have been in by now.'

Jill tried to smile. 'It was stupid of me,' she said. Then with rather a faint laugh, 'We'll know for another time.'

Something seemed to push the *Dabchick* forcibly from behind and Peter looked quickly round. The ensign of the

staff was not trailing behind, but fluttering against the back
of the after cabin. The wind was driving the waves up behind them now and blowing from the north-east. This meant
that the sea would be helping rather than hindering, but it
also meant that there would be no shelter from the shore.
Added to this he realised that if anything should go wrong
the wind could quickly drive them ashore, so he turned to
starboard and stood off from the land once more, even
though this brought the sea more on to the beam.

'I'm afraid we can't help the rolling,' he said. 'But we're
well up on to Audresselles already. That place with the line
of hotels is Wimereux, and from there it's only a couple of
miles. Then I vote we tie up and go into the town and take
ourselves out to lunch.'

'That's a grand idea,' agreed Michael. 'Let's have snails.
I've always wanted to go to France and have snails.'

Even the mention of snails was almost too much for Jill
at that moment. 'I don't know that I shall be feeling very
hungry,' she said in a rather subdued voice.

'Oh yes, you will,' said Peter as he leaned against the side
of the wheelhouse to steady himself. 'You'll see. As soon as
you have firm land under your feet you'll want to eat a
horse.'

Jill tried very hard to laugh, but eventually what was in
her mind had to come out.

'Is it very far on to Le Havre, Peter?'

'Oh, about a hundred miles, I think.' He guessed what
was behind her question. 'Of course we won't go on until
it's really good weather. Then we shall just coast along near
the shore, and if it turns ... er ... choppy, we can always
run in somewhere. If you look at the other chart you'll see
there are plenty of little harbours. Four or five, anyway.
Maybe more.'

By three o'clock Wimereux beach was on their beam and
the pair of massive fortress blocks outside Boulogne lay almost
dead ahead. Peter had folded away the chart and he soon
turned in to run straight up for the harbour jetties, at the

same time taking care to leave a clear hundred yards of water between the *Dabchick* and the end of the northern outer mole which came curving out to sea on the Wimereux side of the town. The big blockhouses lay still half a mile ahead and now somewhat to starboard.

'Nearly there,' he said, steadying the boat with the wheel after a big wave had slewed her with a fierce push on the quarter. 'Ten minutes at the outside, and then –'

'Look out!' It was Michael who saw the black nose of a rock appear for an instant in the trough of a wave only a few yards to one side of the bows. In the same instant Peter saw it too and then another on the other side. There was no room to turn but he threw the engine into reverse and opened the throttle wide. But just at that moment a big sea rolling up behind lifted the *Dabchick* on its shoulder and heaved her forward, carrying her swiftly on.

Fearfully the crew stared ahead through the windshield as the boat rushed forward in spite of the engine's effort to draw her back. To one side a mass of stone broke the surface just ahead of the wave as they ran past. Then quite suddenly the wave dropped and they were in comparatively calm water.

Instantly Peter realized what had happened and he changed to full speed ahead, then eased down once more as the line of rocks drew away astern.

'That was luck,' he said in a rather husky voice. 'But we're in.' He handed the wheel to Michael, unfolded the chart again and examined the approach to Boulogne.

'Yes,' he repeated, 'that was luck, right enough. If it hadn't been for that obliging wave we would have been on top of the mole. Look.' He pointed with his finger and Michael and Jill bent down to see. 'That outer mole runs right round to those blockhouses, only here where it is marked with a dotted line it's all broken down.'

Michael glanced astern. 'You can see it quite clearly now, Peter,' he said. 'See how the waves are breaking along the line of it, right out as far as the forts.'

'You mean to say that we came right over the top?' Jill asked.

'Yes. The entrance is up there between the two block-houses. But we're right inside now. Another time we'll look at the chart more carefully. It would have been a nasty mess if we had struck on top of the wall with those seas breaking on it.'

They were soon running gently up between the big jetties. Off to the right lay a long basin with several cargo ships lying against the wharves. To the right of a pointed jetty in the centre of the harbour the car ferry *Dinard* was moored up to the embarkation quay, but ahead and to the left lay a collection of fishing craft.

'Ease off, Michael,' said Peter. 'Take her up on those fishermen somewhere. There, that one with the saint on the mast, the *Saint Jacques.*'

He slid open the door of the wheelhouse and went forward with Jill for the ropes. An old fisherman with a drooping grey moustache and wearing a faded blue tunic and blue trousers and black wooden clogs nodded to them and took Jill's line.

'Mauvais temps,' he said, jerking his head towards the sea.

'Oui,' said Jill rather self-consciously. 'Mauvais temps.'

'C'est toujours la même chose.' He passed the line through the thwarts of the *Saint Jacques* and took a turn round a bollard before passing back the end. 'Mauvais temps. Pas de pêche. Pas de l'argent.' He put his hands in his pockets and leaned against the gunwale where the nets lay piled in an untidy heap. 'Oui, c'est la vie.'

Jill felt much better after a cup of coffee and three horse-shoe-shaped rolls that were neither quite bread nor entirely pastry. Michael stuck to his determination to sample the snails and he kept assuring the others as he ate them that they were absolutely wonderful, but Peter was more con-servative in his tastes and settled for a couple of poached eggs. They sat for a while in the café before returning to their boat, for the crossing had proved a greater strain than they had realized. At last, however, Jill as quartermaster paid the bill and they walked back towards the fish quay.

Instead of being on the outside the *Dabchick* was now hemmed in by a tangle of fishing-boats, some moored sideways, others bows inwards or stern first in a disorderly mass. Baskets of coal and ice were being lowered from the quayside and boys were tramping across the boats with fish baskets, oil drums and fuel cans. The *Dabchick*'s crew climbed down the oily quayside ladder and threaded their way across the fishing craft, stepping over a maze of lines and nets and gear on the decks until they reached their own boat.

'Let's get out of this,' said Peter as a couple of fishermen clanked over the top of the *Dabchick*'s cabin with sacks of coal for their prawn coppers. 'We won't have any peace while this is going on, and if they suddenly decide to put out to sea in the middle of the night we shall be bumped and crushed and pushed around.'

'We could go over the other side,' Jill suggested. 'There's plenty of room there.' Apart from a dredger and a smart business-like ocean trawler the long quay opposite was unoccupied over its whole length.

'Start her up, Michael. Jill and I will clear these ropes and push the fishing-boats aside to ease her out.'

Nobody seemed to pay much attention to them as they moved the lines from one craft to another. Most of the fishermen were busy with their supplies and the rest just stood or sat on their decks watching impassively.

'Right, Michael. Take her back gently,' called Peter. 'I'll lift the lines of the fishing craft over the wheelhouse as you go.' The water swirled up from the *Dabchick*'s propeller, bringing with it a stench of oil and fish and foul mud.

Michael eased gingerly out with Jill and Peter pushing off on the two sides of the boat, and as soon as they were clear he swung the helm over and ran across to the jetty opposite. A big railway locomotive lay panting at the head of a dark-green train on the quay above, and a few railway porters in blue cotton jackets peered over the edge of the quay as the *Dabchick* turned and drew alongside.

'Tie her up on the baulks of the jetty,' called Peter to Jill. 'Then I'll go up and we can moor her properly. It's a lot quieter over this side.' He put the bow-line round a concrete pier, made fast, and went aft to help her. Michael turned off the engine and came out on deck.

A shrill blast on a whistle made them look up. Hurrying along the edge of the quay above was a man in dark-blue uniform and with gold braided rings stretching from his wrists almost to his elbows. He shouted and blew on his whistle alternately as he came to the head of the ladder above.

'No stop, no stop,' he shouted down. He gesticulated to-wards the harbour entrance. 'Big ship come. *Canterbury*, she come here.' He blew a few more blasts as though letting off steam.

'All right, all right,' muttered Peter. 'Keep your hair on. We'll move.' He went back to the bows. 'Take her off, Michael, stern out first.'

Michael started up the engine and slipped into reverse. It ran for a second or two and then there was a snap and a splash as a rope hanging down from the side of the quay parted and fell into the water. The engine gave a curious jerking shudder and stopped.

'Go on, Michael,' Peter called as the harbour official shouted down to them in a string of voluble French.

Michael started her up again, put the gear to astern and the engine stopped dead. He repeated the performance, this time with the gear set ahead, and once more the engine stopped.

'Allez, allez,' roared the officer, and blew three times on his whistle.

'Oh, go away,' said Michael. He leaned out and called to Peter. 'There's something wrong. The propeller seems jammed, or it may be the gears.'

'Are you sure? Let me see.' Peter pushed into the

wheelhouse. He too started the engine, speeded it up and put the gear in gently, but with the same result.

Jill ran up to the wheelhouse. There was a loose rope hanging over the quayside, she said. 'It broke and fell in when Michael started up. Do you think that's anything to do with it?'

'I'm afraid it is,' Peter answered, remembering a time on the Thames above Henley when the stern line had been left trailing overboard and had got wound round the propeller. The effect had been just the same then. He stepped out on deck again, followed by the others.

'Allez!' screamed the harbour official, waving his arms frantically. '*Canterbury* she come. Boomf!' He made a violent gesture in the air and blew on his whistle with bulging cheeks. 'Allez, allez, vite!'

'Sorry,' Peter called up. 'We can't move, because . . .'

The man drowned him with shouting. The porters stood idly by, taking no part in the scene.

'I wish he would shut up and let us explain,' said Peter. He put his hands to his mouth. 'There is a rope round the propeller, round the hélice,' he shouted, but with no effect at all. 'The man might as well be deaf,' he remarked.

'I should think he is,' laughed Michael. 'I expect he's burst his ears with his own racket.'

'We must do something, Peter,' said Jill, trying to be practical. 'If there's a ship coming here we must move somehow.'

Peter glanced down the harbour. 'She isn't even in sight,' he said.

'I wish he would fall in,' said Michael as the man leaned over the edge and blew shrill blasts at them without ceasing.

'You go, you pay plenty monny,' roared the man in a brief interval between blasts. 'Plenty, plenty monny.'

'Shut up,' said Peter under his breath.

'Throw him a line and pull the end just as he catches it,' suggested Michael with a grin.

A little open fishing-boat came chugging round from be-

hind the steamer quay. The harbour official blew away on
his whistle and yelled to it, pointing at the *Dabchick*. The
man at the tiller shrugged his shoulders and made to run
past the *Dabchick* with the official blowing his lungs out
ashore, but as he drew level Peter called to him, waving a
rope. The fisherman put his tiller over and drew alongside.

'Sur l'hélice,' Peter explained. 'Comme ça.' The man
looked puzzled at first, but suddenly seemed to understand.

'Oui, oui. Oui, oui.' And he reached up for Peter's line
and tied the end to a cleat on his stern.

'Vite, vite!' roared the officer. But the fisherman shouted
back at him. Then he sat down in his own boat and folded
his arms.

'Crétin!' he exclaimed nodding his head towards the
official. 'Beaucoup de bruit, oui?' He smiled at Peter, pulled
a whistle out of his pocket, and blew blasts at the man on the
quay.

'How long does this go on?' Jill asked as the two men
furiously tried to outblow each other. But Michael did not
answer. He darted below and emerged again with his own
scout whistle and the ship's dinner-bell.

'Ah, bon!' exclaimed the fisherman, pausing to draw
breath again. 'Bon! Tout l'orchestre!' He stood up and
blew till his face went a deep red, whilst Michael waved the
bell violently above his head and blew on his own whistle.
Peter put his hands to his mouth and hooted like an owl, and
Jill attempted to whistle but she was quite unable to do so
for laughing.

Suddenly the official stopped his gesticulations, turned on
his heel and stalked off. The porters watched him, but still
did not move.

'Aha!' exclaimed the fisherman, panting. 'A nous la
victoire!' He leapt aboard the *Dabchick*, shook each of the
crew energetically by the hand, jumped back into his own
boat and took up the strain on the rope. As the *Dabchick* trailed
slowly behind towards the fishing-quay the Channel boat
Canterbury came between the forts into the outer harbour.

Tied up again on the outermost fishing-boats Peter thanked the fisherman. 'Payer?' he asked.

The fisherman shook his head. 'Non, non. Vous Anglais. Moi, Français. Nous amis, oui?' He held up his hand and Peter bent down and shook it.

'Oui,' he said. 'Oui. Et merci.'

'I think France is going to be fun,' laughed Michael as he waved to the little fishing-boat. 'As far as I can see you either shout the other fellow down and see who can stick it out longest, or else you're like long-lost brothers.'

'What are we going to do about the propeller?' Jill asked.

'Get the rope off, I suppose,' Peter answered not very enthusiastically with a glance at the surface of the water. The oily blackness was broken here and there by the bobbing fish-heads thrown overboard from the fishing craft.

'You can't possibly go over the side in this filth,' said Jill. 'I could. I've got a bathing cap.'

But Peter shook his head. 'No. I'll have a go. You put on a bucket of water for me to have a wash in afterwards. And Michael, you get out the hacksaw and tie a light line on it so I don't lose it, and put a rope for me to hang on to.' He went below to the after-cabin and soon emerged again in his bathing trunks.

'It smells pretty good,' he grinned as he began to lower himself down the rope. 'I shan't want any more fish for supper.' He let go and disappeared beneath the water.

The line was twisted well and truly around the blades of the propeller, round the rudder bracket and the guard as well. Peter explored carefully in the dim light underneath the stern, keeping one hand on the rope which Michael had let down. Fortunately the obstructing line was not a very thick one and it would not be too difficult to cut it, he thought. He surfaced, reached up for the hacksaw, took a deep breath and submerged again. Holding the keel with one hand he hacked away at the line where it passed tightly over the propeller shaft just ahead of the blades. Half a dozen good strong cuts and the line was severed.

It only needed another dozen dives or so for Peter to un-wind the turns from the shaft and blades, and the rest of the rope then came free when he surfaced and swam on his back to pull at it. Hanging the main piece of it round his neck he hauled himself back aboard, hand over hand. Jill helped to pull him over the catwalk.

'Well done,' she said.

'You've no idea how funny you look,' said Michael. 'There's black stuff all over your back.'

'I'll bring up the water,' Jill said, 'and you can wash on deck. I'll get out a big towel too.'

Peter told Michael to take the *Dabchick* out right away and try round the corner down in the basin they had seen on their way in. As he scrubbed the oil off his arms and Jill sponged at his back Michael turned past the car-ferry quay into the broad expanse of water flanked by warehouses. Down in the bottom corner lay an assembly of lighters, pile-drivers, muck-boats and odds and ends of craft of all des-criptions. Michael brought the *Dabchick* up neatly outside the lighters and himself jumped down with the lines.

'This should do us,' he said as he moored up the boat. 'And with luck we'll be away tomorrow morning.'

Jill rubbed Peter's back with the towel. 'You've been such a magnificent skipper that you can lie up here in the sun,' she said. 'I'll make a cup of tea.'

'And I'm going to bait the line and try for some eels,' said Michael. 'They would be lovely for breakfast tomorrow.'

The corner where they had moored was sheltered from the wind, and Peter lay down on the towel in the warm sunshine.

'I wonder which is most likely to be caught,' he thought to himself as he closed his eyes. 'The bullion thieves by Dad, or the eels by Michael.'

4. Down on the Keel

'There goes another,' Michael exclaimed as he watched the freighter aircraft through the window in the rear of the wheelhouse. 'That's five in less than half an hour.'

The fat-nosed plane was dropping down to circle over the estuary of the Canche and disappear behind the line of hotels which ranged along the waterfront of Le Touquet.

'Only about fifteen minutes out of Lympne, and you're there in France, car, luggage and all,' commented Peter glancing back from the wheel. 'It makes the *Dabchick* look pretty slow.'

'I wouldn't mind flying over like that,' Michael went on. 'All the same, it can't be as much fun as on a boat.'

'Particularly when it's as calm as it is today,' agreed Jill.

The weather could not have been better. The *Dabchick* was running south in brilliant sunshine on water so calm that the surface was silky in its smoothness, and not even the slightest heaving remained to suggest that only the previous afternoon the same sea had been thrown into a confusion of sharp waves and foaming breakers on the French side of the Channel.

'We're making good time,' said Peter, glancing at his watch. 'It's just two hours and fifty minutes since we left Boulogne entrance, and we're nearly down to Berck-sur-Mer. We've got a bit of tide behind us and we should hold it for a couple of hours more.' He shaded his eyes with his hand to cut down the brilliance of the glare from the sun as it sparkled off the smooth water.

'It's a pity Mummy isn't here,' said Michael. 'She would have loved it on a really calm day like this. Hello – there goes another car freighter back to England.'

Jill too watched the aeroplane for a moment before turning to look ahead. 'There are lots of boats out there,' she said pointing just to starboard of the bows. Three or four miles off shore the sea was dotted with the shapes of the small boats of the Boulogne fishermen.

'I expect they're netting out on the banks,' Peter said, pointing with his finger at the chart. 'They're off the Somme Bay.'

'I'm sorry I didn't catch anything in Boulogne,' said Michael regretfully. 'There must be fish there, surely.'

'I doubt it,' said Peter. 'In the outer harbour perhaps, but where we were lying the water was a bit dirty.'

'Well, I'll catch something before long,' Michael assured him. 'Couldn't we put a line over here and trail it behind?'

Peter shook his head. 'We're moving too fast, and I don't think we should slow down just to fish. While we have this good weather we had better make the most of it. It may not go on for ever, and if we keep flogging along we might make Fécamp by supper-time, and even get to Le Havre tonight if we're really lucky.'

'I hope we do,' Jill agreed. 'Once we're there it doesn't matter what the weather's like.'

'Not a bit,' said Peter. 'It can blow a gale when we're in the Seine if it wants to. We shan't mind.'

Little by little the flat coastline edged by sand-dunes passed by on their beam. There was Berck, with its mass of hotels staring blankly out to sea, then the low wooded shores of the mouth of the Authie river and beyond that another few miles of featureless dunes. Far ahead a dark-capped white line showed where the sandy coast gave way to sheer and dazzling cliffs of chalk beyond the Somme Bay. At the southern point of the bay itself a tall thin lighthouse in red and white stripes marked the corner of the channel into Saint-Valery-sur-Somme.

'Pointe du Hourdel,' said Peter, checking it on the chart. 'That lighthouse is about half-way between Boulogne and Dieppe. Rather more than half, actually.'

Michael stared ahead. 'I see a buoy,' he exclaimed, pointing straight over the bow. 'Look, there.'

'That must be the Somme entrance,' said Peter. He laughed. 'It's certainly encouraging to find the buoys really turning up where they're marked on the chart. We'll keep outside that one, as just inside it the sand dries right out and there are quite a few wrecks marked.'

'There's a boat inside all the same,' Jill remarked.

'Why not? It isn't low water,' Michael said. 'They're probably fishing.'

'She isn't moving, anyway,' said Peter. 'She's pointing out towards the buoy but not making up on it.'

'Probably at anchor,' Michael suggested.

'Perhaps, but if so she's in a foolish place.' Peter half closed his eyes to cut down the glare. 'She looks to me like a yacht. We shall pass within two or three hundred yards and then we'll get a good look at her.'

Whilst they ran up towards the buoy the other boat still did not seem to move. They could see her plainly now, a smart little white motor yacht of perhaps thirty feet over all, just a few feet less than the *Dabchick*.

'She hasn't got an anchor down,' Michael decided as they drew nearer to the buoy. 'And . . . I say, look! There's something up. Look at that chap on the deck.'

Now that the *Dabchick* was no more than a quarter of a mile away a man appeared standing near the bows waving above his head a flag on a short staff.

'That's an American flag on the stern,' exclaimed Jill. 'I wonder what they want. Hadn't we better go and see?'

'I'm not going to run around in this bay,' said Peter decidedly. 'Just look at the chart. The whole thing is a mass of banks and flats drying out at low water.'

'But we must,' Jill objected as the man on the yacht continued to wave. 'They aren't more than two or three hundred yards inside the buoy. And just imagine if we were in some kind of trouble and another boat passed by without even bothering to ask what was the matter. You can't just run past them, Peter. Really you can't.'

Peter saw the sense in what his sister said. 'All right,' he said, turning the wheel to port. 'We'll go in and see. I suppose we must, really. But there's quite a flow running across and into the bay – look at the way it's streaming past the buoy there.'

Michael shaded his eyes. '*Marguerite*,' he said slowly as he made out the name on the bows. 'She's rather a super boat.'

Now that the *Dabchick* was no more than a hundred yards away the man on the deck of the white yacht stopped waving the ensign and picked up instead a line ready to heave. Peter eased down and turned a half-circle to bring the *Dabchick* up into the tidal flow a short distance on the *Marguerite*'s beam. Jill and Michael went forward, ready to catch the line.

Peter was leaning out of the wheelhouse door and he noticed that the *Marguerite*'s motor was apparently running for behind the stern the water was being driven back in a turbulent stream. He saw, too, that there were two other figures in the wheelhouse and that one of them, a girl of about Jill's age in a bright check shirt, was at the wheel. The other was a boy of about twelve with a sallow face and straw-coloured hair cut short. He was wearing a gay shirt and tight long trousers.

'O.K.? Here it comes.' The yachtsman flung his line cleanly across the *Dabchick*'s deck.

'They're Americans, all right!' Michael whispered to Jill as he grabbed the line and took a turn round a bollard on the bows. 'But how on earth did they get here?' He raised his voice and called across, 'Can we help?'

'You sure can. We're stuck.' The man pointed out to well behind the stern of his boat, and the crew of the *Dabchick* saw a little black flag on a stick bobbing on a cork float. 'We've got a net fouled up underneath.'

Stepping back to the wheel Peter worked in until only a few feet away from the *Marguerite* and at the same time he cut the throttle down until he was hovering beside her. 'Do you want us to get the line on our stern and tow you out?' he called across.

'Yes. If you can hold us from drifting, then maybe we can cut out our motor and get the net clear. I guess it's round the rudder.'

'Why don't you throw down the anchor and hold her that way?' Peter's suggestion was certainly sensible.

'We dropped the anchor,' the yachtsman answered from the rail. He turned towards his wheelhouse. 'Keep her headed for the buoy, Shirley,' he shouted.

The yachtsman called over to Peter again. 'Yes, we dropped anchor O.K., but the other end of the chain was not made fast aboard the boat.' He saw the broad grin on Michael's face. 'You're right, it was stupid,' he admitted with a short laugh.

'I'll run up ahead and pull on your bows,' said Peter. 'Jill! Bring that line down on to the stern.'

Soon the *Dabchick* was manoeuvred up ahead of the *Marguerite* and Peter took the strain on the rope. He opened the throttle and the water raced out from under the stern. Then he sent Michael aft to shout across that the *Marguerite*'s engine could be stopped.

The man on the *Marguerite* signed to his daughter and the motor was cut. Then the wheelhouse opened and Shirley and her brother came out on deck.

'If you can hold her, we'll free the net,' called the yachtsman to Michael, and picking up a boathook he went to the stern with his two young companions.

With the *Marguerite* straight astern of them it was not easy for the crew of the *Dabchick* to see exactly what was going on, but Michael and Jill watched from the catwalk on either side of the wheelhouse whilst Peter stood at the wheel to keep the boat straight into the tide.

'Honestly,' said Michael. 'Talk about brains. Fancy anybody flinging over the anchor without having the chain shackled on to the boat.'

'I don't know,' said Jill. 'I should think it's quite an easy mistake to make.'

'Lucky we turned up,' said Peter. 'The tide might easily have swept them in and dumped them upon a bank. It might have been just one more wreck to mark on the chart.'

'I wonder how long they've been there,' Jill said.

'Can't have been very long,' Peter replied. 'If it had been when the tide was falling they would have been carried outside the bay, I should imagine.'

There was a great deal of heaving and pulling going on at the stern of the *Marguerite* before the yachtsman came forward to the bows and shouted.

'The boat-hook is stuck fast in the net and we can't pull it out. We've had to drop it. Can you lend us another?'

'What next, I wonder,' whispered Michael. 'I shouldn't lend them our boat-hook, Peter. They'll only get it stuck too.'

Peter considered. 'Jill,' he said, 'run aft and take off the line. I'll drop back and come alongside her and you can tie her bows close in to ours. Michael, put a few fenders down. Then we'll see what we can do when we're alongside.'

As Jill ran back and explained the scheme Peter put the *Dabchick* astern. Both boats had drifted more than a hundred yards farther in before he was alongside, and a glance at the position of the buoy suggested that, even when he had been holding up the *Marguerite* on the engine, the tidal pull on the net and the two boats combined had been greater than the holding power of the *Dabchick*'s motor. He decided to take no chance on drifting farther in to the Somme estuary and so he told Michael to tip the anchor over the bows and let most of the chain run out free. Meanwhile Jill had thrown a line over from the stern to Shirley and was drawing the two craft neatly together.

Peter ran forward and put his hand on the taut anchor chain. There was no vibration, so the hook was evidently holding in the sand. Satisfied, he went back to the wheel-house, turned off the engine, and stepped aboard the *Marguerite* with Jill and Michael.

The yachtsman shook him warmly by the hand. 'Tucker's my name,' he said. 'Say, it's good of you to help us out of this fix. This is my daughter Shirley, and my son Wilbur.'

Rather shyly the crew shook hands all round.

'We were going to Saint-Valery when we picked up the net,' the American went on. 'Guess it's wound itself around the rudder, all right. I've tried all ways to get her loose, and we drifted in nearly a mile before I thought – better hold her or we'll be on the bottom.'

'We'll have a look,' said Peter. 'Our anchor's holding us both up, all right.'

'That sure was dumb, losing ours,' said Mr Tucker as he led the way to the stern. 'You must think us a set of dumb clucks.'

Michael was not quite sure what dumb clucks were, but he was quite prepared to believe it was a suitable term.

'Oh, it can easily happen,' said Jill.

As the party looked over the stern and saw the mass of net with the boat-hook entwined in it, there began a discussion as to how it might be got clear. Wilbur was all for using the *Dabchick*'s boat-hook and trying to haul the net up over the stern, but Peter disagreed.

'The simplest way is to go below with a knife or a saw and cut it adrift,' he declared. 'We had rope round the prop in Boulogne harbour and I cleared it quite easily from below.'

'I wouldn't take a chance on going over, not in this tide,' declared the yachtsman.

'You could hang on to a rope,' suggested Jill.

'Or Wilbur could have dived over,' Michael hinted with a quick challenging look at the other boy. 'I'm sure he could have done it.'

'He's no swimmer,' said Mr Tucker. 'Nor is Shirley.'

'We are, Pop,' objected Wilbur. 'I can swim a hundred yards easy and Shirley can do a quarter-mile back-stroke.'

'Sure, but that's a lot different from diving under the keel.'

'I'll go under,' volunteered Jill.

'So will I,' said Peter.

'It's my turn,' Jill objected. 'You had your go at Boulogne. Please let me, Peter.'

'All right. But only if you have a rope round you. I don't want you to get mixed up in the net.'

'There's nobody goes diving under my boat,' said the American firmly. 'Cut the net from on board, yes; but diving under, no.'

'We might get at it with our dinghy,' suggested Michael.

Peter shook his head. 'We couldn't reach far enough underneath. No. It's a matter for diving, that's definite.'

'Well, none of us is going to dive under,' asserted the yachtsman vigorously. 'And I'll not have any of you risking getting messed up in that net. We've got into this fix but we'll get out of it somehow.'

'But how?' asked Jill. She really wanted to dive.

'Couldn't you lash a knife to their boat-hook and chop the net away, Pop?' wondered Shirley.

Peter decided to take charge of the situation. 'Listen,' he said. 'We can't stay here all day. I don't like hanging about among these banks, for one thing; and besides, we're on our

way down to Le Havre and we want to get there. We can't
tow you with the net dragging, that's certain. If you're to get
out of this bay the most sensible thing is for somebody to
dive –'

'It's not safe,' said the yachtsman.

'It's perfectly safe,' Jill objected. 'I don't mind going
down. In fact I would like to.'

'Can't I help?' Shirley too seemed to want to get things
moving.

'You can get a rope,' said Peter. 'We'll tie it round my
sister's waist when she goes in.'

Jill went below in the *Dabchick*, slipped into her swim-suit
and bathing-cap, and returned armed with the bread-knife.
She stepped over to the far side of the *Marguerite*, let Peter
tie a loop of rope below her arms, and stood ready to jump.

'You're not going over there, young lady,' said the yachtsman. 'Down behind the stern is different, maybe, but –'

'Go on, Jill,' broke in Peter. 'I've got the line.'

And before she could be prevented, Jill dropped neatly
over the side and Peter let the line run out through his hands.

'Pull her out, man. Pull her out!' Mr Tucker started to
grapple with the rope. 'It's sure good of her to try but I'll
not have people taking risks on my account.'

'Leave her alone,' said Peter firmly. 'Jill knows what she's
doing.'

Almost at once Wilbur shouted from the stern. 'There
goes the net!' Down below in the clear water the net was
carried swiftly away in the tide and Jill broke surface just
level with the stern.

'Done it,' she cried.

Michael clapped his hands and so did Wilbur. Shirley and
her father leaned over the side to reach for Jill's arms as
Peter belayed the rope to keep her from drifting down.
Putting the bread-knife between her teeth like a pirate she
reached up and was quickly hauled aboard.

'I don't know how to thank you, young lady,' began Mr
Tucker. 'Was it caught round the rudder?'

'Er . . . yes,' Jill panted. 'That's right, round the rudder right close to the stern. It only needed a hack or two and away it went.'

'That sure is fine of you,' Shirley said. 'I don't know what we would have done. I'm no diver myself.' She led Jill below and produced a towel. 'I'm sorry my Pop was so unpleasant about your wanting to dive,' she whispered. 'He's sweet, really, only he once had a friend drowned spearing fish under water in Florida. Guess it makes him kind of nervy. He never likes Wilbur and me even to swim where we can't stand. And I can swim well too, though I can't dive like you can.'

Jill smiled. 'That's all right,' she said. 'I understand perfectly. Please don't worry.' She rubbed her arms and Shirley dabbed at her legs. 'I'll explain it to Peter too, because I think he seemed a little annoyed. Thanks for the towel.'

She ran up on deck, where the yachtsman once more thanked her and the other members of the *Dabchick* crew. He started up his engine and Peter's party stepped back aboard their own boat.

'Where are you for?' Peter called back.

'We don't know,' Shirley answered with a wave. 'Maybe Havre anyway for a start.'

'Probably see you somewhere,' Peter replied. 'Have a good run. We'll haul up anchor and be on our way too.'

The boats were cast off from each other and as the *Marguerite*'s party waved farewell and ran out for the buoy Michael ran the *Dabchick* up on the anchor and Peter hauled in the chain.

'Right away,' he called as the anchor came to the surface. 'Full speed ahead.' And they turned their backs on the Somme estuary to make up for the buoy by which they had come in.

'Peter,' said Jill seriously as soon as they were all in the wheelhouse. 'That girl Shirley asked me to explain that her father is nervy about people diving because a friend of his was drowned fishing under water.'

'I see,' said Peter. 'That explains a lot.'

'It was a bit thick, all the same,' said Michael with his eye on the buoy.

Jill spoke very earnestly. 'Peter,' she said, 'what that girl told me isn't true. It was just to put us off the scent. You know I said the net was caught on the rudder? Well, it wasn't. I just said so to pretend I hadn't noticed anything. The net was caught on the Chesterfield gold. I saw it.'

'What!'

'I don't believe it,' exclaimed Michael. 'You've got gold on the brain.'

But Jill was serious. Just about six feet or so ahead of the propeller, she said, the netting was caught over a projection. She had slashed the net away, and as it drifted back she had seen a couple of dull golden bars, held to the side of the shallow keel with a pair of screw things.

'You know,' she said. 'Those hook-shaped things carpenters use.'

'You mean clamps,' said Michael, staring at her in astonishment.

'Yes, clamps. And I'll tell you what else. I could see quite plainly a kind of circle on each, and the letters R.G.C. all sort of run together.'

'Robert G. Chesterfield,' said Peter slowly. Then very seriously, 'You're not fooling us, are you, Jill?'

She shook her head. 'Of course not. I wondered what to do, but I thought it best to come up quickly as though I had seen nothing.'

'Quite right,' said Peter.

'I'm not surprised he was so anxious that you shouldn't go diving underneath,' Michael said.

'I know. But what do we do?'

'Keep sight of them at all costs,' said Peter. 'Keep about this distance away, Michael, and we'll follow them. When they run into harbour we can see what has got to be done.'

'Do you think the two children know?' Michael asked.

'Shirley does,' Jill pointed out. 'She wouldn't have taken

me below to explain her father's behaviour if she hadn't known the real reason.'

'All the same she seemed to want you to go in,' said Peter, puzzled. 'Somehow I don't think she knew. Probably her father tipped her off to apologise for him.'

'I'll tell you another thing,' Michael said. 'They seemed in a great hurry to be off without bothering to wait for us. And it's most suspicious that they're Americans.'

'But why should anybody suspect people just because they're Americans?' reasoned Jill. 'They're no more suspicious than anybody else.'

'Well, it was American gold,' Michael argued.

'H'm. That's true.'

'I must say it's a jolly clever way of taking the stuff over to France,' said Peter. 'They must have set out from somewhere in England, and no doubt their boat was thoroughly searched, just as ours was. Only not on the keel.'

'Do you think we should send Daddy a wire in Paris? He'll want to know at once,' Jill said.

Peter considered. 'I doubt it,' he said. 'They're not likely to suspect that we know what they're up to, and provided we don't lose sight of them we stand a good chance of seeing where they deliver their little cargo.'

'Besides,' Michael agreed, 'we are on friendly terms with them. We can go out of our way to talk to them and all that sort of thing. It won't look a bit odd if we stick close to them, and we might be able to pick up some hints as to where they've come from and where they're going. I expect they're bound for the Seine in any case.'

'Well, they're heading south now, right enough,' said Peter as he watched the *Marguerite* running ahead of them off Cayeux. 'If they go on day and night we'll have to do the same. We've plenty of fuel to get us farther than Le Havre if need be. But whatever we do we mustn't lose them, and we must not let them suspect for one moment that we are being anything else but just friendly.'

An hour later the *Marguerite* swept in between the Dieppe

piers, still a couple of hundred yards ahead of the *Dabchick*. Wilbur waved from the stern rail and Michael answered with a toot on the hooter.

'I wonder if they could get away from us out at sea if they really tried,' he said as he ran up the long curving sweep that led to the basin.

Peter, however, was satisfied. 'We can hold them,' he said. 'If they were going flat out, as I should think they were, then there's no chance of them giving us the slip later.'

'Well, now we're here I think we should tell the police,' Jill said. 'Or we could phone a message through for Daddy.'

'No,' said Peter decidedly. 'They've only a small part of the gold hidden on the keel. There's not likely to be any more inside the ship because of the thorough searches in England. It looks as though the *Marguerite*'s job is to carry the stuff over in batches and get rid of it. If we can find where they take it, and where they fetch it from, then we may at least stand a chance of helping Dad to find the whole lot, and the thieves, too. But once we have the *Marguerite* stopped and searched, the thieves will be warned and they'll find some other way of bringing the gold over.'

'I suppose so,' said Jill. 'Only it would be a pity if we lost the chance of helping Daddy.'

Michael slowed, and turned into the basin right in the centre of the town. Two Channel ferries lay round to the right, and along the opposite wall the *Marguerite* was just drawing in beside a ladder. Wilbur waved, beckoning the *Dabchick* alongside.

'Suit us fine,' whispered Peter. 'We can keep an eye on them there.'

Jill went on deck and picked up a line.

'Catch!'

'O.K., I got it.' Wilbur took a turn round a stern bollard and lobbed the end back to Jill. Then he ran forward and took a second line from her at the bows. Meanwhile his father was climbing the uneven rungs of the rusty ladder with the nooses of a pair of lines over his shoulder.

'I'll go up and help him,' Peter muttered to Michael. 'I want to make sure he doesn't speak to a soul without one of us being at hand.'

He stepped across the *Marguerite* and followed up the ladder. 'Please,' he said courteously as he reached the quayside. 'Give me one of the lines and I'll take it up to that bollard ahead.'

'Thanks a lot,' said Mr Tucker, handing over one of the lines and slipping the other over a post on the quayside. 'Well, if it hadn't been for your help we wouldn't be here at all. We might still have been up there off Saint-Valery. I sure am grateful to you, and to your sister, too. She's a fine girl, and I'm truly sorry I was just a bit rough the way I spoke when she offered to dive in.'

'Oh, she's not a bad diver really,' agreed Peter. He moved along the quay, dropped the noose over a bollard and came back again. 'Are you staying long at Dieppe?' he asked innocently.

'Only tonight. Tomorrow I hope to make Havre and then perhaps run to Cherbourg in a day or two. We've no fixed plans.'

No, thought Peter, they've no fixed plans. They'll wait and see how they can best get rid of us. That's their first job.

Almost without thinking he was noting a detailed picture of the American so that he could pass it on. The man was tall, probably about five feet eleven inches, eyes blue, hair dark but greyed, close-cropped. Thin on the whole, and with a rather pale complexion. Wearing white trousers, a blue nautical jacket, a braided yachtsman's cap with an enamelled badge showing a blue flag in a wreath, blue-and-white yachting shoes, a shirt of salmon colour, shiny like nylon. Peter imagined the description going out over the radio.

Casually he asked another question. 'Is she your own boat?'

'Mine?' The American laughed. 'No, she's not mine. I've a yacht down in Florida but you wouldn't find me sailing her across the Atlantic. No, this little tub I hired for six weeks down near Southampton. We only left yesterday.'

Peter thought hard. 'How did you come to be up at Saint-Valery if you were heading for Cherbourg?'

'Ah, that,' Mr Tucker smiled. 'That was Wilbur's idea. He wanted to see Saint-Valery on account of the great man who sailed from there. I didn't know he put out from Saint-Valery.'

Puzzled, Peter could think of nobody connected with Saint-Valery. Probably it was some American or other, he thought.

'Well,' he said, 'who was it?'

'Why, William the Conqueror. Our family came from England just over a hundred years ago, so naturally Wilbur wanted to see where William sailed from.'

'Oh yes,' Peter agreed. 'Naturally.'

'And if we hadn't got strung up we would have made it, too,' the American added. 'But by the time you were along to help we had missed most of the tide, so I guess we'll have to leave old William out of it for this time'

Peter was calculating hard. 'You must have left England in the dark, then,' he suggested.

'Sure. Round about eleven o'clock last night we put out from the Hamble river.'

Making a mental note Peter wondered whether or not this information was true. 'You preferred to cross at night, then?'

The yachtsman nodded. The tides happened to be favourable, he explained, and as he didn't know the French coast he preferred to sail for lights which he could identify from their various individual flashes. 'Of course they had to delay us for nearly an hour,' he added. 'Call it Customs searching – why, they nearly pulled the whole ship to pieces. I've never been treated like that in my life before and I don't intend to be again, either. I'm going to sit right down and write to our Embassy in London. Yes, sir. Anybody would have thought we were crooks, the grilling they gave us.'

'I'm sorry,' said Peter. 'I know the customs people are sometimes suspicious. I expect it was just because you left at night.' He decided to slip in another question. 'I like the look of your ship,' he said. 'She's got good lines, too. Did you hire her privately or from a yard?'

'I got her through an advertisement in *Yachting* – that's a magazine published in the States. She's private, but the hiring was handled by a yard on the Hamble.'

'Oh, Cox and Jones's, I suppose,' suggested Peter inventing a name to draw him out.

'No. Blagdon Brothers is the name,' said Mr Tucker easily. 'And talking of names, I haven't the pleasure of knowing yours.'

Peter thought hurriedly and bent down to fiddle on the rope as though adjusting it. The trouble was that Michael and Jill might be answering the same question down at the bottom of the wall, and he had no idea what they would be saying. Obviously they ought to have discussed this matter of their name before reaching Dieppe, but it was now too late. By nature Peter was scrupulously truthful, but he knew it was important not to risk being identified in any way with his father. Anybody involved in the bullion theft would be perfectly well aware of the name of the man directing the English end of the hunt, for it had continually been in the papers, and if Peter admitted to being a Branxome the American's suspicions might be roused. On the other hand, a false name could lead to difficulties too, particularly if any telegrams from his father were delivered to the boat or if they had to produce their passports when the Tuckers were present. And if the Americans were to find that they had concealed their proper name they would at once be suspicious. He decided that honesty involved fewer risks, and as he answered he hoped that Michael and Jill had taken the same decision.

'Branxome,' he said. 'It's quite a common name,' he added hopefully.

'Branxome, eh? Branxome. Well, I'm pleased to meet

you, Mr Branxome, and most grateful for all your help. Are there just the three of you aboard?'

'Yes,' Peter replied. 'There's just me – that's Peter – and Jill and Michael.'

'I'll just call you Peter,' Mr Tucker said. 'And now I've a surprise for you and your crew. I want you and Michael and your sister to come out with us and we'll have dinner this evening in the town, all the six of us. You did us a real good turn today, and I would like you to be my guests. No,' he said as Peter began to protest. 'No, I won't take No for an answer. We'll make it a real party.'

Peter mumbled his thanks and hoped that any lack of enthusiasm in his voice would be mistaken for shyness.

'Come on, then,' said the American, moving to the top of the ladder. 'We had better be getting back aboard to tell the others that there's to be a celebration. After you, sir.'

The moment Peter reached the *Dabchick* he dashed below to discuss some means of ensuring that at least one of them could drop out of the party and stay aboard. It was absolutely vital that the *Marguerite* should not be left unwatched, and though of course Mr Tucker's invitation was only natural under the circumstances, Peter was certain that it had really been made as a means of drawing them away whilst an accomplice came and retrieved the gold bars from the keel. 'Dashed cunning,' he said to himself. 'We weren't likely to refuse – and in decency we couldn't, anyway.'

He burst into the fore cabin, to find Jill and Michael and Shirley and Wilbur all assembled together, talking and laughing.

'Oh, Michael,' he said. 'Sorry to interrupt everybody like this, but could you er . . . come with me and er . . . check the fuel.'

'I'll help,' said Wilbur eagerly.

'No, no. Please don't.' Peter meant it even more than his voice suggested. 'It's quite all right. Michael and I can manage.' And he succeeded in extracting Michael, who guessed very well that he was wanted alone.

Peter led him aft. 'Look here, have they asked you your name?'

'Yes,' whispered Michael. 'I quickly said "Wilson" before Jill had a chance to give the show away.'

'I knew this would happen,' sighed Peter. 'I told the man I was a Branxome.'

'Well, you be a Branxome, we'll be Wilsons,' said Michael brightly.

'We can't. He knows we're brothers and sister.' Michael was not defeated. 'Step-brother and step-sister,' he said. 'You know, your Daddy died when you were a baby. Fell under a steam-roller,' he giggled.

'Good. That's fine, only no steam-rollers. Make it – let's see, er . . . typhus in India. Tell Jill as soon as you can. Remember now, you're both Wilsons and I'm not.' He dropped his voice even lower and explained the difficulty about the party. 'You've got to stay here at all costs. Feel sick, anything you like.'

'Why me?' Michael objected. 'Why not you? They might treat us to snails.'

'I'll see you get a bucketful of snails in Paris,' said Peter. 'Only you've got to stay and keep watch. If anybody comes alongside, blow on the hooter to attract attention.'

Michael considered. 'Is that a promise?'

'What?'

'The bucketful of snails.'

'Yes, I suppose so.'

'Honestly?'

'Yes, yes. Anything you like.'

'Then I'll stay.' Michael licked his lips. 'I shan't forget the promise, either. Snails are super.'

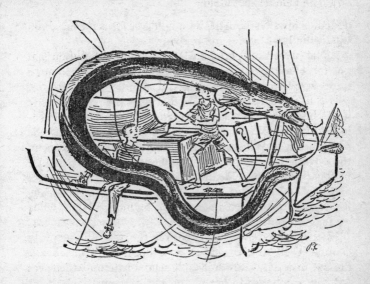

5. Michael Gets Busy

Michael was enjoying his evening enormously. At first he rather resented the way Peter had cut him out of the evening's party by ordering him to stay aboard the *Dabchick* to keep watch, and even the thought of Paris and the promised abundance of snails in parsley butter did not completely restore his usual cheerfulness. But he was too anxious to prevent the loss of the gold bars from the *Marguerite*'s keel to think of disobeying his skipper's orders, and so as soon as the subject of the supper was broached he dutifully declared that he would prefer to stay on board. He was tired, he said, and not at all hungry – though this was far from true. He would prefer to remain on the boat and just sit about. Really he would much rather, he said. He would probably just go off to his bunk and sleep. Or perhaps, he added as an afterthought, he might fish for a bit first, and watch the boats across the harbour.

As he played his part he tried to sound enthusiastic and not to behave like an unwilling martyr, but he was quite unprepared for what followed.

'I'd like to stay too, Pop,' Wilbur declared. And whether it was because Mr Tucker was glad to have somebody keeping an eye on Michael, or – as Jill thought – because he really believed Wilbur and Michael would prefer to spend the evening together, Wilbur's father at once agreed.

'That's not a bad idea,' he said at once. 'You stay too, and you and Michael can make yourselves a meal on the *Marguerite* if you like. You can entertain him on board while we four are out.'

Michael stood beside Wilbur as the rest of the party clambered up the ladder to go ashore. Mr Tucker was dressed in a light-grey suit with a broad tie on which was painted a sailing-ship heeling on the starboard tack. Peter had on clean flannels and a jacket, Jill a cotton frock and walking shoes, and Shirley had put on a gay nylon dress with a flared skirt. She had a neat little bag too, and Peter carried it up the ladder for her so that she had both hands free for the rungs. Michael could not help smiling when he saw Peter pull a clean rag out of his pocket up on the quayside, and hand it first to Shirley and then to Jill and Mr Tucker so that they could wipe the oily dirt off their hands after climbing the greasy rungs of the ladder.

'That's Peter all over,' he thought to himself. 'Always trying to be polite. Even though he knows the Tuckers are crooks he runs around after them like a nursemaid. When Daddy has them arrested, Peter will probably want to see that somebody takes them breakfast in bed in the cells. He won't catch me making such a fool of myself. If I've got to spend the evening with this Wilbur boy I'll pretend to be friendly so that he doesn't suspect anything, but that's all. I'm not going to make a fool of myself. Crooks are crooks, and they don't deserve help from anybody.'

Wilbur suddenly interrupted his thoughts. 'Let's have a coke,' he said as the party disappeared.

'Coke?' Michael was puzzled indeed.

'Sure. Coca-cola. Come on.' And he led the way into the galley which was a little smaller than that on the *Dabchick* but otherwise much the same.

Wilbur opened a locker and pulled out a couple of bottles which he opened. Michael surreptitiously smelt the fizzy liquid that was handed to him, and sipped it cautiously. It was not quite like anything he had tasted before and he wouldn't have known quite how to describe it, but it was not unpleasant.

'Like it?' Wilbur asked as he saw Michael trying the taste.

'Sure,' said Michael with an effort to talk as the occasion demanded.

'How about something to eat? Or if you're not hungry we can give supper a miss.'

Michael said that on the whole he thought he was hungry after all, and he offered to scramble some eggs. But Wilbur declared it was the host's job to do the cooking. He would make a couple of Hamburgers for each of them, and they could take them up on deck. Certainly Wilbur proved an excellent cook, and when at last he had his delicacies ready and they sat up on the bows to eat them Michael was genuinely enthusiastic in his praise. He had rarely tasted anything so good, he said. And he really meant it. Perhaps Wilbur might not be so bad after all, he thought. And of course there was just a faint chance that he really knew nothing about his father's gold-running activities.

When they had finished, Michael had an idea. No, he was not softening, but what harm could it do to enjoy the evening with Wilbur so far as such a thing was possible? Besides, it was a sheer waste of opportunity just to lie moored along such a promising harbour wall and not take advantage of the fact.

'Let's see if we can catch some eels,' he suggested. Wilbur was not sure that eels were really worth catching – not like the tunnies they had hooked off the coast of Florida from his father's sailing-boat. But he was prepared to take Michael's word for it, and before long he was helping to bait the hooks that projected from the little wire sidearms on the tackles which Michael fetched over from the *Dabchick*.

'Bacon fat,' said Michael, throwing a couple of broad rashers down on the deck. 'Bacon fat, that's the stuff. Eels can't resist it. To them it's as good as . . . well, Hamburgers.' And laughing they set to work to thread the big lumps of white fat on the hooks.

'Do we throw the lines out?' Wilbur asked as he held one ready.

'No. Lower them down over the side, right close to the wall. That's where the eels will be if there are any. They always poke about by the walls.'

As soon as one line was ready they dropped it over the side and set to work on the next, until at the end they had four lines down with a total of twelve barbed hooks. They made themselves comfortable with one line in each hand.

'If you feel anything, pull firmly but don't jerk,' advised Michael. 'If there are eels here we'll get them all right.'

For a minute or two they sat staring down towards the water and waiting.

'Are your folks at home?' Wilbur asked the question suddenly.

Michael wondered quickly whether this might be a catch but he decided it was not. After all, he and Jill were supposed to be Wilsons, not Branxomes. 'Daddy couldn't get away just at the moment, and my mother has gone to visit her sister in Scotland,' he said. 'So we started ahead and they'll both meet us somewhere later. I don't know where or when,' he added cautiously.

He was not anxious to get entangled in awkward questions about his relationship to Peter, so he turned to the matter of the voyage. 'Where are you bound for?' he asked.

Wilbur explained that they really didn't know. His father intended first to run as far as Cherbourg, and then he thought they would probably cruise around on the Brittany coast for a couple of weeks. They would just go where it suited them, and then . . .

Suddenly Wilbur pulled one of his lines and stood up. 'Quick! There's something there. I'm sure,' he exclaimed.

Michael dropped his lines. Sure enough, Wilbur's line was taut, and moving sideways through the water. 'Haul it in steadily,' Michael instructed urgently. 'Haul it in till you have him on the surface, and then . . .' Wilbur was already pulling up his line. The first two hooks appeared down below the side of the boat and then there came a splashing as the third came into view with a fine silver eel hooked through the jaw. The creature was lashing out, flicking his tail right over his head and twisting it round the line.

'I know what,' Michael exclaimed quickly as they peered down at the catch. 'Pull him down aft, then swing him up right over the side and drop him in your dinghy. He can't get out of that.'

Carefully Wilbur drew his line along the side of the boat whilst Michael pushed out from the wall to leave more room. Then as Michael stood clear Wilbur lifted the line and swung it inboard. With a writhing and flapping the eel was safely dropped in the *Marguerite*'s dinghy and at once burrowed into a coil of rope, twisting in and out and covering it with sticky slime.

'He's a beauty,' said Michael gleefully. 'Must be at least a couple of pounds. There's breakfast for three of you on him, easily.'

Michael knew that eels were difficult customers to handle, apart from being horribly greasy, and it would be quite a job to handle this fellow and remove the hook. So he advised Wilbur to leave the eel to quieten down for a few minutes while they returned to their lines.

'They're best smoked,' he added. 'But you'll have to have him fried, which is just about as good, really.'

'I've an idea,' exclaimed Wilbur. 'We've a stove in one of the cabins. See – there's the stove-pipe. What d'you say we light up a fire and hang him in the stove-pipe? We've got some coal.'

'I think it has to be wood,' said Michael dubiously.

'O.K. Look, you keep a hold on these lines and I'll go up on the quay. I'll find some wood – you see if I don't.' And handing over his lines Wilbur climbed swiftly up the ladder.

He wasn't away long. Within a few minutes he had collected together a few broken fish boxes and some pieces of packing-case lids from beside the dock railway track and each time he returned to the edge of the quay he waved his new finds excitedly in the air.

'Hooray!' Michael shouted up. 'Here, catch this.' He flung up a heaving line and Wilbur began to tie the end through the slats of a couple of boxes.

'Here they come,' he called as he got them ready to lower down to the deck.

'Wait!' Michael felt something pull on his fishing-line. 'Hang on a moment. Here's another.'

It was not such a big eel this time, but it was well worth catching and Michael drew him down aft and swung him up to join the first in the dinghy.

'Gee,' called Wilbur. 'That's fine. We'll maybe get a few more.'

With eels biting, Michael soon forgot about the gold, and as soon as Wilbur had lowered all his wood and returned on board they decided to deal with the two they had caught so as to free the lines for further use. Michael had read that the simplest thing to do was to nick an eel in the back just behind the head, and whilst Wilbur tried to hold the big one between the coils of the rope he drew out his scout knife and climbed right into the dinghy to tackle it. He didn't like the job, but soon he had both eels cut, and the hooks were extracted.

'You get the fire on, and as soon as I've baited up again and put the lines back, I'll clean the eels in the galley,' he said.

By eight o'clock the wood had been broken up, the fire

was hot and a total of three eels had been caught, gutted, freed of slime by pulling them through a pad of steel wool in the galley, and hung head downwards in the chimney. Michael had found a couple of meat skewers in the *Dabchick*'s galley and Wilbur had impaled the tails and rested the skewers over the top of the chimney pipe.

When the party returned from their dinner ashore it was nearly nine and a soft cloud of pale-blue smoke from the *Marguerite*'s stove-pipe was drifting up over the quay. A fourth eel had just been slipped down the chimney alongside the others.

'Let's not tell them,' whispered Michael as Peter came first down the ladder, ready to help the girls on to the deck. 'Let's see if they notice.'

'Hello, there!' exclaimed Mr Tucker as he stretched across from the bottom of the ladder. 'I see you've got the fire on. You feeling cold or something?'

'We thought it would be nice for Shirley to have her cabin warm,' said Michael.

'Thanks,' Shirley said. 'That sure was thoughtful.'

'I don't suppose you've caught anything,' Peter said.

Wilbur lifted both his lines. 'Nothing there,' he said, trying to sound disappointed.

'Nor on mine,' added Michael, winding his in, too, and putting them on deck.

'Have you had supper?' Wilbur's father asked.

'Rather.' Michael praised Wilbur's cooking, describing the Hamburgers with real enthusiasm.

'We had a lovely time,' said Jill.

'Snails?' Michael asked.

'No. Something much better. First we had some wonderful sort of little soft doughy things all stuffed with mince and covered with tomato sauce.'

'Ravioli,' said Shirley.

'It was lovely,' Jill continued. 'And then we had the Chef's Speciality, thin slices of beef cooked in sauce over a silver lamp right by the table.'

'And wonderful fruit afterwards,' Peter said. 'I've never seen such pears.'

'I'm sorry you weren't along with us,' said Shirley.

Michael darted a glance at Peter. 'I don't mind,' he said. He remembered Peter's promise and had visions of dining in state with tail-coated waiters advancing in procession to his table, each carrying a dish of snails.

'I don't care either,' said Wilbur. 'We've had better things to do than sit in a restaurant all evening. Perhaps you fine ladies and gentlemen will just step this way and see what the real hard-working sailors have been doing while you've been out.'

He led the way aft to the chimney and pointed.

'Smoked eels,' he said proudly amid the general gasps of astonishment. 'Four of them. We caught them, Michael gutted them, and I fixed up the fire.' Carefully he lifted a skewer and showed the two lovely smoked fish hanging from it. 'Smells good?' He waved it gently to and fro under their noses.

'It sure does,' said Mr Tucker. 'It was a good idea, you two staying.' He laughed kindly.

'Nice work,' agreed Peter. 'There's plenty of meat on them, too.'

Wilbur replaced the eels in the smoke. 'O.K. Then we can have them for breakfast.'

'Yes,' said Jill. 'That's a fine idea. And you three can come aboard our boat in the morning and we'll all have breakfast together.'

Before long the two crews parted for the night and the *Dabchick* party gathered in the fore-cabin. Jill drew the curtains and they sat close round the table after Peter had closed the door.

'Only in whispers,' he warned. 'We mustn't be overheard.' The others nodded.

'Well,' Peter resumed. 'What have you picked up?'

'Four eels,' Michael giggled.

'Yes, I know. But what else?'

'Nothing. I didn't have a chance. We were fishing right up till when you came back, and ... Look here, Peter, Wilbur's quite a nice boy. I'm sure he doesn't know anything about the gold.'

'No? Perhaps he's just crafty.'

'I don't think so,' objected Michael with a shake of his head. 'He doesn't seem at all crafty to me. Wilbur is all right, I'm sure of that. I don't think he knows about the gold.'

'I wouldn't be too sure,' Peter persisted. 'After all, Shirley seemed perfectly innocent while we were out, yet you remember that it was she who made the excuses about why her father tried to stop Jill diving. Actually I think she's quite pleasant too.' Seeing the broad grin on Michael's face he stopped. 'What's funny?' he asked.

'Oh, nothing.'

'Well, what's the harm in thinking Shirley's quite pleasant? That's not the same as going all mushy about her. And if you want to know, I think her clothes are a bit too smart for on board a boat.'

'Hear, hear,' said Michael.

Jill tapped on the table. 'Gentlemen, gentlemen,' she said. 'We're discussing the Tuckers, not Peter's opinions on fashions.'

'All right, then, let's discuss the Tuckers. What do you think of Shirley?'

'I like her,' said Jill definitely. 'And I don't think she knows about the gold either. Didn't you notice what she said at supper? She said she would like me to show her how to dive under the keel in case it came in handy again one day. Surely she wouldn't actually invite me to come and do it again if she knew that the gold was there on the keel?'

'I'm not so sure,' said Peter. 'I think it sounds rather fishy. If they've got the gold underneath they'll want to bring it up one day, so it's not surprising if Shirley wants to have diving lessons.'

'What did Mr Tucker say?' Michael asked.

'Oh,' answered Jill, 'he was dead against it. He said diving under boats is dangerous. That's why I think Shirley doesn't know about it. If she was wanting practice to get the gold up later, as Peter suggests, then surely her father would have encouraged her.'

'That's a point,' Peter admitted. 'So up to now we have Wilbur and Shirley both considered innocent, and both agreed to be reasonably pleasant.'

'Wilbur's more than reasonably pleasant,' Michael objected. 'He's all right. I really like him.'

'Anyway, we've dealt with them,' Peter continued. 'What about the father?'

'He's a crook, all right,' said Michael. 'Look at his tie. It's like the ones gangsters wear in films.'

'Actually it's a yacht-club tie,' Jill corrected him. 'He said so.'

'I don't believe it. But even if it is, why shouldn't a crook join a yacht club? It would be quite a good cover for a bit of smuggling.'

'He's certainly a crook,' Peter agreed. 'I expect that when Dad sees him he'll be able to pick out his photograph right away. . . .'

'Peter!' Michael stood up in his excitement. 'Peter, that's just the idea. Listen! I've got my camera on board. It's only a box, I know, but it takes jolly good snaps. Let's ask them to pose for their photos tomorrow morning, and we'll post the film to Daddy at the Sûreté in Paris. We'll tell him about the gold, and see what he says.'

'That's a good scheme,' agreed Peter. 'All the same, I doubt if he'll be keen to have his picture taken.'

'Well, he can't exactly refuse,' Jill said. 'Let's try. And you had better write to Daddy and tell him what we've discovered, and that we're shadowing the *Marguerite* like a pack of bloodhounds.'

'Bloodhounds don't shadow,' said Michael. 'They follow the scent when the quarry has disappeared.'

'Ladies and gentlemen . . .' Peter began.

'I know,' said Jill. 'We're here to discuss the Tuckers, not the habits of various kinds of dogs.'

Before they broke up and turned in for the night the skipper had written a letter with the hindrance rather than the help of his crew, who kept prompting him.

Dear Dad, [it ran] Please get this film developed at once. The people in the picture are on a yacht called *Marguerite*. They say they chartered it. We helped them get a net off their bottom. Jill dived under and found two gold bars with the initials R.G.C. in a circle clamped to the bottom of the keel. We have pretended we didn't see anything.

The man's name is Tucker, or so he says. We think the children probably don't know about the gold. They are all Americans. We are shadowing them and will stick close to them. They say they don't know where they are going, but probably Cherbourg. We are watching them night and day in case they have arranged to deliver the gold somewhere. If you want to get hold of us, I expect the coastguards will know where we are, but please don't let squads of excited French policemen come screaming round us. The Tuckers might notice. – Peter.

ps. – The Tuckers took Peter and me out to supper here. It was lovely. – Jill.

pps. – Wilbur (the Tucker boy) and I caught four eels in the harbour. We are smoking them in the *Marguerite*'s chimney-pipe. I think Wilbur is rather nice. Wasn't it lucky Jill saw it? – Michael.

pps. – By the way, do the Sûreté people give you snails? – Michael.

Peter folded the letter and put it in his pocket. There only remained to arrange the watches. The *Dabchick*'s crew were determined to take no chances on the *Marguerite*'s gold being disposed of during the night, and so it was agreed that Peter would keep a look-out until two in the morning, Jill would take the shift from two until five, and Michael the last watch up to breakfast. There were to be no lights, but the curtains would be drawn back just far enough to see out, and at the least sign of anything suspicious the rest of the crew were to be awakened.

Peter found his watch difficult. He kept on yawning, for the dark made him sleepy. At first he tried to keep awake by dipping his finger in a glass of cold water and moistening his eyelids, but the effect of this soon grew less and less. He tried standing on one leg and even kneeling in an uncomfortable position on the edge of his bunk, but it was only by continually changing from sitting to standing and kneeling that he kept awake at all. He was not sorry when after a time that seemed as long as four nights rolled into one a clock somewhere in the town struck two and he could tiptoe through to see Jill thoroughly awake and watching before he turned in. Then he dropped down on his bunk without even bothering to undress, and in a moment he was fast asleep.

Jill's watch was easier because she had already had some rest. It was shorter too, and the morning light was well up before Michael's turn came round. At about a quarter to four she heard sounds of movement, and, peeping out between the curtain and the window frame, she saw in the dim light Wilbur's head appearing cautiously through the *Marguerite*'s forward hatch. He looked around for a moment, then emerged on to the deck and tiptoed very quietly along the catwalk. For a moment Jill thought of waking Peter, but she stayed where she was to see what was in the wind.

Wilbur climbed gingerly on to the after-deck and went over to the chimney-pipe. Very carefully he lifted up the skewers in turn, looking admiringly at the long slender forms of the eels, replaced them as quietly as he had taken them out, and tiptoed back again to disappear through the hatch. Jill watched him with amusement, but she did not wake the crew.

Michael's watch was hardly a watch at all, for soon after six there were signs of normal life on both boats. Shirley eventually came across to help prepare the breakfast but the actual cooking of the eels was left to Jill, with plenty of advice from Michael and Wilbur who stood watching in the doorway of the galley. The *Dabchick*'s saloon was just large enough for the six of them to sit round the table, and after

Michael had gone ashore for milk and bread they all set to work on a breakfast which was as good as any they could remember.

It was a glorious day without a breath of wind, and the smoke from the ferry boats across the basin was rising straight in the air. Mr Tucker seemed in high spirits and he suggested getting under way as soon as breakfast was cleared, in order to make Le Havre while the conditions were so good.

Peter kicked Michael's feet under the table.

'Oh, I forgot,' Michael said. 'I would love to have a photo of you three on your boat. I've got my camera handy. Would you let me take one or two snaps?'

Rather to his surprise Mr Tucker was quite agreeable. 'O.K.,' he said. 'Anything you like. And I'll take a picture of your craft, too, to send to the folks back home when we tell them how you helped us.'

Michael took two pictures of the *Marguerite*'s crew ranged up on her deck. Then he insisted on taking one of each of them separately, from quite close up. The *Dabchick* crew then took their turn while Mr Tucker got to work with his own camera, and after the portrait session was over they disappeared quickly below decks. Michael wound back the film, took it out, and sealed it up in its box with sticky paper. Jill wrapped the letter round it and put the packet in an envelope, tying it round outside with string for safety. Then she handed it to Peter, who slipped it into his pocket and walked casually across the *Marguerite*'s deck to climb the ladder and disappear into the town. Just for extra precaution he registered the packet and paid for express delivery too.

On his way back to the boat Peter considered their situation. It had been a wonderful stroke of luck finding the gold hidden on the *Marguerite*'s keel, and he could not help admiring the ingenious way in which the bullion was carried out of England right under the noses of the customs officers who, when they searched the bilges, must actually have been within a foot of the two bars. But the one thing that really puzzled him was why only two bars were being carried. At this rate the *Marguerite* would need to make at least fifty trips to carry the entire load. Of course there might be difficulties in disposing of gold in bulk even in France, and perhaps small regular shipments were easier. And there was always the chance that Tucker chartered other boats for the successive trips, or even that several craft were engaged in the smuggling all at the same time, and the *Marguerite* was only one of a fleet.

Those problems, however, were really the concern of his father and the police. At least they themselves had found how the gold was transported, and it now remained to keep a close watch on the Tucker boat and see where they went and how they landed their secret cargo.

So far there had been no difficulty, but an organization bold enough to raid the boat train and detach the bullion van was not likely to be easily foiled by himself and his crew. If necessary the American might use some kind of trick to get rid of the *Dabchick*'s company. Perhaps even violence.

Peter found himself wondering whether the *Marguerite* would dare actually to try to sink them. She had strong pointed bows and if she were suddenly to wheel round and ram the *Dabchick* amidships when they were hidden from the view of the coastguards by the high cliffs, what would happen then? Or supposing Mr Tucker were suddenly to attack him on board and lay him out, and then tackle Jill and Michael, seize the ship and drive it aground? There were so many possibilities, and he would have to be on his guard against all of them.

He was not frightened, but he felt very responsible for the safety of both Jill and Michael. They were a plucky pair, but he could not take any risks which might put them in danger. At the same time it would just be cowardly to lose the opportunity of sticking to the scent of the bullion thieves, and it was quite probable that success in following up this one part of the story might provide his father with the evidence needed to recover the whole consignment. It was almost inconceivable that the *Marguerite* could dispose of its gold,

even at night, without their noticing, and that meant that
sooner or later there might have to be a show-down. Just
what form it might take he could not possibly foresee. The
only thing was to be absolutely alert for the least sign of
danger, and then act promptly.

On the whole, Peter thought that Michael and Jill did not
realize the dangers, and he decided that it would be better
not to share his own worries with them. The calmer they
both were, the better. He had no doubt that they would be
completely reliable when the moment came, and perhaps
Michael would have one of his sudden bright ideas. That
was the remarkable thing about Michael. He was always
having brain-waves, and they were usually very sensible.
His scheme for taking Tucker's picture and sending it to
their father was brilliant but at the same time so simple.
Jill could have thought of it, and so could he. But they
didn't. It needed Michael to see the obvious.

Back on board he found Michael had already scored another success. Beckoning his brother excitedly into the cabin
Michael cautiously opened a locker and pointed. Peter
could see nothing but an empty glass.

'Finger-prints!' Michael exclaimed. 'I took him a little
milk in a glass and said Jill wondered if it was going off.
Could he taste it and see, I asked. And of course he took it
like a lamb, sipped it, and said he thought it quite O.K. I've
got the whole of his right hand at one go. Daddy will be
frightfully pleased.'

Peter grinned with admiration. 'Honestly, Michael,' he
said, 'I don't know how you think of these things. But it's
certainly a good job you're here. It's the next best thing to
having Sherlock Holmes signed on in the crew.'

A moment later they heard the American calling down to
them, and Peter went on deck. Mr Tucker had a proposition
to make, which took Peter by surprise.

'If we're running down to Le Havre together, how d'you
say we split crews? One of you come aboard us, and one of
us will go with you. O.K.?'

'Yes . . .' Peter said hesitantly, trying at the same time to think very hard what was behind the suggestion.

'O.K. Then how shall we fix it? Suppose you take Shirley and we have your sister – how's that?'

Peter considered. If there was any chance of monkey business it would be best for himself to be on the *Marguerite*, but he was certainly needed aboard the *Dabchick* in case of engine trouble.

Wilbur, standing on the bows, heard his father's suggestion. 'Let's take Michael, Pop. He and I are buddies.'

'Yes,' said Peter. 'You take Michael, we'll have Shirley.' Michael was so resourceful that Peter felt quite safe in letting him go with the Tuckers.

'Then that's fixed. Shall we go?'

'Sure. We're ready.'

Peter went below to find Michael. 'You're going with your buddy,' he said with a laugh. 'He wants to swop you for Shirley. Keep your eyes open, and –'

'I'm not worrying,' Michael said. 'I'm quite happy to go on the *Marguerite*. I can take care of myself. Wilbur's all right, and his father doesn't suspect that we know anything.'

Soon the two craft were turning in the basin to run down the curving gulley and out between the piers in the wake of a small British cargo ship. Peter took the lead at once, and when Shirley and Jill had coiled the ropes and lifted the fenders they brought up an armful of cushions and lay in the sun on the fore-deck. Astern, the *Marguerite* followed them and Peter noted that Wilbur was giving Michael a turn at the wheel whilst his father was tidying up forward.

The sea was absolutely flat, and as they ran down off-shore Peter put on his dark glasses to cut down the glare from the brilliant surface of the blue water. He looked at the chart and laid off to starboard towards the buoy opposite the massive headland of the Pointe d'Ailly with its lighthouse perched close to the edge of the great cliffs. The point itself hid the more distant stretch of coastline, but as soon as they were running up on the buoy it was possible to see round the corner to where mile upon mile of majestic white and pinkish cliffs rose up sheer from the water's edge.

Lunch-time brought Fécamp into view. It appeared quite suddenly as they rounded a headland and saw the jetties no more than a quarter of a mile away. The girls, who had been asleep most of the time, went below to bring up a rough-and-ready lunch of corned-beef sandwiches and orangeade. Peter glanced over his shoulder to make sure that the *Marguerite* was not cutting into Fécamp, but she was running straight behind them with the yachtsman at the wheel whilst Michael and Wilbur were sitting on the fore-deck apparently occupied in repairing rope splices.

Jill took over while Peter had lunch with Shirley on deck, and, as the chart showed deep water without obstructions, he dozed off to sleep soon afterwards. When he next awoke, the girls were both in the wheelhouse and the ship was running past a small resort where people were lying out in deck-chairs on the beach.

Jill called forward. 'Can Shirley take her?'

'Certainly. Keep about a mile off, that's all.' And as Jill handed over the wheel to go and deal with the washing-up, Peter went back towards the wheelhouse just to make sure that Shirley had the feel of the boat.

'I wonder,' he said to himself. 'I can't believe she's mixed up in this business, and yet . . .' He opened the door and stepped inside.

'How are you doing?'

'Fine, thanks.' Shirley had the boat on a steady course, and by the way she handled the wheel Peter had no doubt at all that she was competent.

'A couple of hours should see us at Le Havre,' he said.

'Good.' Shirley stared out ahead, her eyes narrowed to cut the glare.

'Here, take these,' Peter took off his glasses and put them on her.

'Thanks, Peter. Say, that sister of yours is a swell girl.'

'Jill? Oh, she's all right.'

'I like her,' Shirley went on. 'Quiet, but she's got plenty of sense. There aren't many girls I know who would have dived under like she did yesterday. My Pop thought she was wonderful, too.'

Peter murmured something about Jill always having been fond of diving.

'Well, maybe she is. But I like her, anyway. We've been getting on fine while you were asleep up there.' She paused, and glanced at the chart. They were slowly making up round the great headland and the tide seemed to be slackening. 'I think it's fun being together like this,' she went on. 'It's far better than just being on our own. Couldn't we team up and all go some place together? I would like to, and I know Wilbur would. What do you say?'

Peter really did not know just what to say. If the Tuckers were content to have them around it certainly made things a lot easier. On the other hand, there might be a catch in it somewhere. But he had to admit that Shirley was not likely to encourage them to come along if she knew about the gold.

'It might be quite an idea,' he said rather indefinitely. 'We'll have to see what your plans are, and how ours fit in with them.' He pointed ahead. 'That's the Cap de la Hève,' he said. 'Le Havre is only just round the corner. Would you like me to take a turn?'

'I'm O.K., thanks. I like being at the wheel. I like your boat, too. She's fine.'

'Then I'll stay here too, and you can tell me about the United States,' said Peter. 'I've never been there.'

Jill came up again and joined them in the wheelhouse. Shirley took up Peter's invitation and began to tell them of her own country. They lived in Brooklyn, she said, up on the Heights looking over the East River towards the downtown section of New York with its crowded blocks of skyscrapers. She told them about the Empire State Building, and the Statue of Liberty, about Broadway with its gay lights and theatres, Fifth Avenue and the great stores and fashionable shops, and about Rockefeller Centre with an ice rink outside and acres of gardens on the roof. Everything sounded magnificent and impressive, and she was still telling them of the wonders of her own country when the shape of a big ship came slowly into view, apparently coming right out of the cliff.

'The channel must be right in round the point there,' said Peter with another glance at the chart. 'Close the land a bit more, Shirley, and run her round about a quarter mile off the lighthouse there.'

Immediately round the rocks of the point the suburbs of the great port began. A buoyed channel swept slowly round behind the headland, and in another twenty minutes they were shaping up through the roadsteads towards where a mole jutted out from the northern shore of the estuary.

'Now to find a berth,' Peter said. 'Can I take her?' Glancing in over the mole he saw the masts of numerous sailing yachts, and he turned round behind the pierhead and slackened speed to let the others make up.

The *Marguerite* closed in astern and the two craft ran gently up the cut into a great sheltered basin, the inner side of which ran off into a sandy beach. The water was dotted with yachts of every size and description moored in lines to buoys. Shirley scanned the harbour carefully and then pointed.

'In there, Peter. Round the back and up the third row. There are two empty berths there side by side. I'll go forward and reach down for the buoy.'

'I don't think you'll be able to reach,' said Peter. 'We can drop the dinghy.'

'No,' said Shirley. 'I've a better idea. Jill can drop the line over and I'll jump in and tie her up. Then I'll swim over and fix the *Marguerite* too.'

She dashed down below and soon reappeared in her swim-suit. As Peter manoeuvred the bows up to the buoy she poised herself on the edge of the boat. The water looked very far below her, but she was not afraid to try to dive, even

D

though it was the first time in her life that she had done so. Shutting her eyes she plunged forward and down.

The loud smack and the sheet of water flung up on deck indicated that the dive was not exactly perfect. But Shirley did not mind. Though smarting down her front she called to Jill to throw the rope, and soon the *Dabchick* was moored up.

Peter put over a rope ladder and waited to help her aboard again when she had taken the *Marguerite*'s rope too, and passed the end through the ring on the neighbouring buoy.

'Well done,' he said with a smile, leaning down to take her arm. 'I knew you would be a really useful member of the crew.'

'It wasn't much of a dive,' Shirley laughed. 'But you just wait. Give me a couple of days more, and I'll do better.'

Peter turned off the engine and stood on deck. Already Michael and Wilbur were busily baiting their lines on the deck of the *Marguerite* a few yards away. Mr Tucker was standing at the rail and he lifted his hand in a friendly wave.

'I'll drop our dinghy,' Peter called. 'Then we can go ashore.'

Jill and Shirley were lying out on deck again and Peter was just lifting the dinghy on its davit when there was a gentle bump as a small row-boat drew up against the stern. A fat round face topped with a beret appeared over the counter.

'You go to Paris?' asked the stranger in the curious clipped sing-song which the French use when speaking English. 'I am the grocer. I bring you bread, meat, vegee-tables, cigars, wines, liqueurs.' He scrambled aboard, pulled out his order book and drew a pencil from behind his ear.

'Jill,' called Peter. 'Here's real service for you. The grocer is here, waiting for your order.'

6. *A Misunderstanding at Night*

'You go to Paris, yes?' The ship chandler repeated his question.

'Yes,' said Jill. She did not want to say that they hadn't decided, in case Shirley should think it suspicious. 'Yes, we're going up the Seine.'

'Then you have a nice trip. The Seine it is beautiful, very beautiful. It takes you three days to Paris. Where did you come from – Newhaven, no?'

'We came from Dover,' said Jill. 'We crossed to Boulogne and came down the coast.'

'Ah, that is beautiful too. And the weather is good for the sea.'

The chandler at last got down to business and produced long lists of provisions printed in English and ranging from manila ropes to sirloin of beef and boxes of matches. Jill passed over the endless varieties of wine and looked through the list of groceries. She decided to stock up again with bacon and butter, eggs and bread, fresh vegetables, fruit and salad.

The man took down her order and closed his book with a snap.

'Tomorrow morning, mademoiselle, at seven – that will be soon enough?'

'Oh, quite,' Jill said. 'I don't expect we shall be leaving till midday, and certainly not before nine.'

The chandler bowed and scrambled back into his boat. A few strokes of his oars took him over to the *Marguerite*.

'Good evening, sir.' He climbed aboard with his book and lists. 'You go to Paris too?'

'We're making down for Cherbourg,' said the American.

'Ah, so you do not intend to visit the Seine? It is very beautiful.'

'I guess we'll just cruise around in Brittany,' Mr Tucker answered.

'Ah, yes, I see. And now, sir, can I have your order? I am at your service.' He opened his book and handed over the lists.

When his business was completed, the chandler eventually rowed away to the end of the basin, and the crews of the two boats planned their evening jointly. The girls decided on a bathe and then Peter and Shirley would go ashore and look around. Mr Tucker seemed quite content to stay aboard the *Marguerite*, and Wilbur and Michael installed themselves fore and aft on the *Dabchick*, complete with their eel-lines.

'I don't know that it will be so good here,' Michael said. 'Up against walls is always best for eels, and here we're right out in the basin. Still, there might be something else, you never know. We might pick up some flat fish, only I'm not sure what bait they like best.'

The evening soon slipped by. When Peter and Shirley at last returned they reported that the town was not particularly interesting. It had been heavily damaged during the war, and even now it looked battered except where great new buildings were going up. There was nothing picturesque about it. Le Havre was definitely a commercial city.

Evidently there were no eels either. Michael thought he once felt a bite, but when he pulled at the long line there was nothing on it, though some of the fat had apparently gone. Still, neither he nor Wilbur were inclined to give up hope, and they insisted that after dark the eels might turn up from somewhere or other. You never could tell with eels, they explained hopefully.

Supper was on board the *Marguerite*, with Shirley as chief cook and Jill as assistant. And it was during the course of the meal that Shirley again suggested a joint voyage of the two ships and their crews.

'I think it would be fine if we went together,' she said. 'It would be much more sport than on our own.'

'Hear, hear,' agreed Michael.

'But, Shirley,' said her father, 'perhaps our friends here may want to be by themselves. They have their own plans.'

'They're going to Paris,' she answered. 'Why couldn't we go to Paris too? I've always wanted to see Paris.'

Mr Tucker smiled. 'Well, I guess that's O.K., but what about asking them?'

Peter was surprised that the American was so easily prepared to change his plans. Previously the *Marguerite* had been bound for Brittany, presumably to deliver the gold in one of the little fishing ports round the coast or even at Cherbourg itself. How, then, could Mr Tucker suddenly be willing to go to Paris instead?

Two explanations came to his mind. The first was that the American had always intended to run up to Paris – after all, wasn't that where the gold had begun to turn up? If so, then the story about Cherbourg had just been put out to keep the real destination secret, but now that Mr Tucker found the *Dabchick* bound for the Seine he could no longer stick to his original story because the *Dabchick* would almost certainly see him on the way up river.

The second possibility, and a much more alarming one,

was that a change of plans really did not matter. And if this were so it could only mean that the gold was to be landed here, in Le Havre, before they set off together next day as was now being suggested. If this were the intention, then real vigilance would be needed all through the night, and Peter decided to keep the dinghy on the water and have it ready for immediate pursuit if anybody came out to visit the *Marguerite* in the dark.

Turning these things over in his mind he was hardly aware that both Wilbur and Jill were enthusiastically supporting the scheme of a joint run to Paris. Then suddenly his own turn came.

'How about you, Peter?' Shirley looked at him with an encouraging smile.

'Oh, yes,' he said, trying to make his voice sound quite natural. 'I think it's a splendid idea.'

'Then that's agreed,' Mr Tucker said. 'We'll go places together.'

Everybody was sleepy after a day of sea air and sunshine, and as it was already getting dark by the time the supper things were washed up and cleared away the crews separated for the night, the *Dabchick* party rowing over to their own boat in their dinghy. Within half an hour all the lights were out on the *Marguerite* and Jill and Peter turned in, leaving the first watch to Michael.

There was no doubt in Michael's mind as to how he would occupy himself. Creeping quietly up on deck he examined the baits on the lines and dropped all four of them softly over the side, two at the stern and one on each quarter. As the weight pulled each line down towards the bottom a streak of pale-green sparkles flashed in the water, and Michael watched in fascination. He had never seen phosphorescent water before, and as soon as he had placed all his lines and tied them to the rails he picked up the boat-hook and stirred the surface gently to make rings of bluish-green light ripple out and die away almost as soon as they had formed. He tried writing his name with the point of the hook, and then he dipped the pail overboard and amused himself with pouring little glittering cascades from his hands back into the bucket again.

From time to time he remembered to make a tour of inspection of his lines, but no eels seemed to want to take his juicy pieces of bacon. On the whole he was not surprised because he hardly expected eels to be as abundant out in the yacht basin as they were alongside the stone walls of Dieppe. Of course he was a bit disappointed, but he persevered just the same, and, in his determination not to miss a bite, he eventually untied the lines from the rails and led each of them over the cabin top to behind the wheelhouse. Settling himself comfortably with a cushion he leaned back against the rear of the wheelhouse and stretched out his legs till his feet rested on the forward chock of the dinghy rest. He drew each line taut and took a turn round one of his fingers, so that in the event of a bite he would know which line to pull.

He was perfectly content to sit there in the warm summer night listening to the faint lapping of the wavelets in the entrance of the basin and gazing out towards the lights ranged on the hills which rose up behind the town. He would have liked to go for a row round the harbour, but he knew that he was supposed to be on watch. And besides, that way he might miss an eel.

Not that watching was very hard work. The *Marguerite* was lying only a stone's throw away. Her dinghy was still slung inboard, and the American could not possibly launch it undetected. Nor could anybody row out to visit him without Michael hearing, or perhaps seeing the phosphorescent trail which even the most silent oarsman would surely leave behind him.

Michael had thoroughly enjoyed his day's voyage on the *Marguerite* and Wilbur's father had been a pleasant skipper and more competent than Michael had expected after the exhibition in Somme Bay. He had allowed Michael and Wilbur to run the ship between them, and his own contribution to life on board had been to produce the lunch and to regale Michael with tales of fishing for tunny and other monsters in the Florida Gulf.

All in all, Michael thought that the American was rather nicer than a crook ought to be. But this did not really surprise him, for time and time again his father had stressed that the really successful thieves and swindlers were the ones who were so pleasant and friendly and polite in their contacts with other people that nobody could really bring themselves to suspect them. Crooks who crept about with their hats pulled over their eyes, and their coat collars turned up like film gangsters, never had much of a chance. People just took one look at them and dialled 999 on the telephone. The most successful ones were those who mixed freely with other people, joined a golf club in order to discover who had a gold watch worth stealing, offered their seats to ladies in the bus or tube in order to be thought courteous and considerate, or cultivated interesting conversation to throw their victims off guard.

'If you find yourself getting on really easily with somebody, then the chances are he's a crook,' his father had said. 'If he isn't, then he's most likely a C.I.D. man who's making friends with you to try and discover whether or not you yourself are a crook. Of course there's always a possibility that he really is just an ordinary chap and neither a criminal nor a police officer, but there's no harm in being on the look-out.'

Michael, too, was puzzled at the readiness with which Mr Tucker had been willing to change his plans. He agreed with Peter's possible explanations hurriedly whispered just before the first night watch began, but another possibility now occurred to him. Perhaps Mr Tucker was not delivering the gold at all. It might be his share, a reward for some part he had played in the train robbery, and he was just carrying it around with him until there was some opportunity of disposing of it.

As he stared out at the reflections of the city lights on the smooth surface of the yacht basin, Michael gradually began to feel drowsy. His head nodded and his eyes simply refused to stay open. Although he tried for all he was worth to keep awake, he eventually dropped off to sleep, the eel lines still twisted round the fingers of his left hand.

It was after one o'clock in the morning when he was rudely and painfully awakened by a wrench at his arm which made his shoulder joint crack. One of the lines tightened round his finger so forcibly that he only just managed to prevent himself from yelling. Half scrambling, half dragged towards the rail he dropped the other lines and held on for all he was worth.

The yacht basin was not very deep, and, although the tide was now rising, the depth of water under the rows of little ships was still only eighteen or twenty feet. Peering down over the rail as he braced himself to take the strain, Michael could see the water rippled with the thrashing of whatever had taken the bait down below, and through the tremors on the surface he noticed the dim glow of phosphorescence shining faintly upwards from where the creature was moving as it pulled forcefully on the end of the line.

Luminous sparkles covered an area larger than himself, and though he could not make out the shape of the monster he had hooked he could at least see that it was far too broad for an eel. Instead of being long and thin and twisting, the lines of phosphorescence seemed to spring from the sides of a body which he estimated at five or six feet in length at least and perhaps a couple of feet broad.

Straining at the line Michael endeavoured to haul it in, but the monster proved too strong for him to hold, and to prevent himself from being dragged over the rail he had to pay out a further length. He could have belayed round a stanchion but he felt certain that if the line were held rigidly the strength of the creature would snap it.

Names of powerful beasts of the sea ran through Michael's head. Tunny, barracuda, all Mr Tucker's fine fish of Florida – but surely not here in this harbour. Besides, Wilbur's father had painted most graphic pictures of the way these big fish rushed and lunged when hooked, whereas his own prize seemed to move more slowly, just pulling. Could it be a giant squid? Or a seal? Bubbles came up from it, but it never broke surface to show him its true shape and he had to pay out still more line. A shark perhaps, he thought, one of those small harmless ones that were sometimes hooked on the south coast of England – though if it were a shark it would surely lash out, or bite the line.

'It would be super if it was a sturgeon,' he said to himself excitedly. 'And a female one too with buckets of caviare.' He had seen pots of the delicacy in a smart London grocer's window marked, 'This week's bargain. Caviare, only nineteen and six an ounce.' He had no idea what caviare tasted like, but the sheer fun of eating a few pounds' worth for breakfast would make the taste unimportant. Or he might sell it on the quayside. . . .

Michael had almost decided that it would be a sturgeon when the pulling stopped abruptly and the line dropped slack. Quickly he drew it in, hoping once more to feel the strain, but his prize had vanished. As the end of the line came over the rail he found it severed above where it had been connected to the traces. The tackle was gone.

Of course it was a great disappointment, but there was no point in worrying about it. He knew that he could hardly have hoped to hold the creature for long, and landing it on board would have been almost impossible. If only he had called for help Peter might have woken up and come to his assistance. Perhaps Peter could even have speared the giant with the boat-hook. But it was too late now.

The sudden relaxing of effort made Michael aware that he was tired and rather cold. He looked at his watch, and realizing that he had exceeded his spell of duty by more than an hour he wound in the remaining lines, laid them on the deck and disappeared down the companion ladder. Then he woke Peter.

'Anything happening?' Peter asked with a grunt as he opened his eyes.

'No, not really.'

'What do you mean, "not really"?'

'Nothing. There's nothing happening.'

'I suppose you've been fishing all the time,' Peter said. 'Did you catch anything?'

'No, not really.'

'Well, surely you either did or you didn't,' Peter objected as he swung his legs over the edge of his bunk.

Michael had really wanted to keep his adventure secret, but already Peter's interest was aroused. 'I suppose you hooked a big one and it got away,' he said. 'Is that the story?'

'Yes. It took the tackle and everything,' Michael said. 'It must have been absolutely colossal.'

'I expect you fouled the buoy chain,' said Peter. 'I don't imagine there are any fish worth troubling about in this harbour. You had better get to sleep.'

'It was a fish, honestly,' said Michael, rather annoyed. 'The water here glows when it's disturbed, and I saw its shape. It was bigger than me.'

'Nonsense,' said Peter.

'It was,' persisted Michael. 'I could see it.'

'All right, then, it was. Perhaps it was an elephant fish.' Peter laughed sarcastically as he pulled up his tie. 'I expect you fell asleep and dreamed the whole thing.'

'I didn't.' Michael said no more, but climbed into his bunk. He ought to have kept quiet, he knew. People never believed stories about big fish that got away. Still, one day he would hook a really big fellow and land him, and then Peter would see what he could do. Meanwhile he would not tell the others what had happened. Except Wilbur, perhaps. He would tell Wilbur next day if they were alone together. Wilbur would believe him, he felt sure.

Next morning, true to his word, the chandler came rowing out from the shore, bringing with him the grocery orders, and after breakfast the two craft dropped their moorings and left the basin to move up to the entrance lock of the Canal de Tancarville. They were obliged to wait for lock gates, swing bridges, lifting bridges, and a railway bridge, so that the afternoon had half slipped by before at last the ten miles of cut opened out unobstructed ahead of them, running across the marshes of the estuary at the foot of a steep range of chalky hills. When finally they reached the lock where the canal ran out into the river upstream of the treacherous banks of the estuary they found themselves behind a solid mass of waiting barges.

'Never mind,' said Peter as he brought the *Dabchick* up on the mooring piles and waved for the *Marguerite* to draw alongside. 'Once we're through here there's nothing to stop us. We can moor up somewhere for the night, and tomorrow morning we can get cracking again. According to the map it's about eighty-five miles up to the first lock on the Seine, and if we get the tide under us we should make good time. There's not a single bridge of any kind until Rouen, and that's a good sixty miles up river, so we shouldn't have a lot of trouble.'

The barges ahead were mostly tanker craft from the refineries along the canal banks. Heavily laden, they were not easily manoeuvrable, and the time slipped by as they were taken into the lock and tied up in rows of three until the space was nearly full. In the corner beside the gates there was just room enough for the *Marguerite*, but Mr Tucker declined the lock-keeper's offer, preferring to wait until the next batch when there would be ample space for the five remaining barges and both yachts as well. Peter was relieved that the *Marguerite* was not going to pass through ahead, as the lock took so long to fill and empty that he might never have been able to overtake the other boat once it had disappeared up river with a couple of hours' start.

They had been only a few moments in the lock when Jill noticed that Mr Tucker had left the *Marguerite* and was crossing the lane behind the quay. He seemed to ask something of a man selling vegetables from a cart, who pointed to a small group of houses. Mr Tucker nodded, quickened his step and disappeared into the door of one of them. There was a letter-box outside, and on the glass of the door Jill saw the word *Postes*.

She moved back to where Peter and Michael were sitting on the stern.

In spite of himself Peter stood up quickly. 'Are you sure? Where?'

Jill explained without looking round.

Quickly Peter moved to the bows. 'Hallo, Wilbur,' he called. 'Didn't your father go ashore? He mustn't get left behind when the water drops in the lock. Shall I go and find him?'

'He won't be away long,' Wilbur called back.

'Where did he go?' Peter hoped it did not sound too inquisitive.

'Only to the post-office. He's gone to cable our change of plans, so we get our mail sent to Paris. Shouldn't take him long. Look, here he comes.'

As Mr Tucker emerged from the village post-office Peter went aft again to join Jill and Michael. In low voices they discussed what had happened.

'We ought to have been able to stop that,' Michael said.

Peter shook his head. 'I don't see how. We couldn't have prevented him.'

'I wonder what he really did in there. It looks a bit suspicious.'

'Couldn't have been telephoning,' Peter said. 'He was out too quickly.'

'He didn't post a letter in the box outside,' Jill said. 'I was watching.'

'Then probably he really was sending a telegram, just as Wilbur said.'

'Yes, but to whom?' Michael asked.

'It might have been to anybody. It might have been to say that he was on his way to Paris with the gold.'

'Or just to have their letters forwarded,' Jill said. 'We can't find out.'

'No. We'll just have to be on the watch more than ever.'

'I think we should tell Daddy.'

'No,' Peter said decidedly. 'He already knows we're shadowing them. We don't want the French police to come and mess everything up.'

'Hear, hear,' agreed Michael.

'Look out,' whispered Jill suddenly. Mr Tucker was walking along the quayside to adjust the ropes above them.

'I just cabled my bank in London to forward our mail to Paris instead of Cherbourg,' he said. 'Handy finding a post office right here.'

'Yes,' said Peter, watching him closely. 'Very handy.' He moved to the wheelhouse ready to start up the engine when the water had dropped to the level beyond the lock.

The whole party was becoming impatient with the slow progress of the day, and when at last the huge gates swung back to allow them to run out into the channel of the great river they were relieved to know that at last the way would lie open before them. Peter led out to cut across the muddy water towards the opposite shore, but the sight of a big cargo vessel sweeping down river on the falling tide made him wisely decide to keep to the near side until she had passed. Then, with the *Marguerite* only fifty yards behind him, he crossed the stream and turned to head for Paris.

The river course turned a bend to the right opposite the massive castle of Tancarville, and Peter hugged the bend as close as he dared in order to take the water where the tide ran less strongly. But even there the pace of the ebb was so great that neither of the yachts was making up river at more than a couple of knots. Peter eased down and beckoned the *Marguerite* to draw up on the beam.

'There's no point in punching up against this stream,' he called across. 'I think we'll do best to anchor round beyond the bend and wait till we have the tide behind us tomorrow. What do you say?'

'O.K. by me,' Mr Tucker shouted back.

Scanning the shore line, Peter noticed some heavy piles

a short way off shore and he nosed up to the second one, so that Jill could drop the noose of the bow-rope over it. Then he dropped back towards the pile astern, and Michael managed to fling a great loop of a heaving-line over it in order to haul the stern rope round the post and back on board again.

The *Marguerite* drew alongside, and with fenders between them the two craft lay snugly together on the *Dabchick*'s bow-line. Peter turned off the engine and he had just stepped aboard the other craft to help Shirley moor up the stern a little closer when one of the barges which had left the lock behind them began to draw level. The skipper was holding the big wheel with one hand and waving his other to and fro.

'Pas là, pas là,' he shouted.

'What's the matter with him?' muttered Mr Tucker.

'Pas là!' called the Frenchman. 'Le Mascaret arrivera pendant la nuit. Boom!' He made a gesture of an explosion.

'I don't catch what he was shouting about,' Peter said in a puzzled voice.

Jill rather prided herself on her French. 'He said that the Maskeray is coming here during the night – boom!'

'What's the Maskeray?' asked Shirley.

'Why, a ship, of course,' said Michael. 'These are its moorings, I suppose.'

'Well, why can't it push off and go somewhere else. We got here first,' Wilbur said.

'H'm. That's true. All the same, we don't want to be smashed up in the night,' Peter pointed out. 'If the ship is coming in here then I suppose we must move. Better be on the safe side. We can pull in somewhere else just a short way ahead, I imagine.'

Reluctantly the two boats cast off again and moved upstream. Half a mile farther on Peter noticed a pair of oil jetties on the opposite shore. There were no ships lying alongside, so after waiting to let a big tanker come down the centre of the river he moved across and drew gently up against the first of the piers. Once more the *Marguerite* came up on the outer side and tied up.

Twice whilst supper was being cooked down below decks barges punching upstream hooted long and loud. On the first occasion the barge-master shouted something which nobody heard and then passed on his way with a deliberate shrug as though he had done his best but to no avail. The second time, however, one of the deck-hands on a smartly painted tanker-craft stood on the bows and signalled with his arms in semaphore.

'Quick, Michael,' Peter called. 'There's a chap signalling.'

Michael stuck his head out of the hatch, then scrambled on deck. 'M-A-S-C-A-R-E-T,' he spelled out. 'Mascaret.'

Peter waved to show that he had understood. 'They seem to have the thing pretty well on their minds,' he said. 'I wonder why there's all the fuss.'

'Oh, just because they're French,' Michael said. 'French people can never go on without a lot of fuss and bother. Remember that harbour man at Boulogne?'

'Yes.' Peter laughed. 'Still, this must be a gigantic ship if they're all so excited about her.'

'Are you sure it's a ship?' Wilbur asked. 'I thought Mascaret was that stuff Shirley puts on her eyebrows when nobody's looking.'

'I don't,' Shirley objected. 'And anyway, that's mascara.'

'You don't, but it's mascara. That's rich,' Wilbur giggled. 'Ow!' He jumped as his sister kicked him under the table.

'It's a ship,' said Michael. 'It must be. But there's plenty of room over here. The other jetty is free, so I don't see why we should bother.'

'We can always move up if necessary,' said Peter.

Neither Mr Tucker nor Shirley nor Jill were anxious to stay up and watch for the arrival of the *Mascaret*. Nor was Peter. They were all too sleepy after a day which had consisted for the most part in waiting. Michael and Wilbur were equally sleepy but they had enough curiosity to insist upon staying on deck until midnight. So after the washing-up was finished and the others had one by one turned in for the night they got out the fishing-lines again and baited up hopefully with fresh pieces of bacon from the stores which the chandler had brought aboard that morning.

The last of the ebb-tide traffic had ceased by this time, and everything on the river was quiet. The two craft, moored side by side, rocked ever so gently in the curious rhythmic ripples caused by the turn of the tide. Wilbur sat on top of the *Marguerite*'s after cabin, a line in each hand, whilst Michael lay beside him stretched out flat, each of his middle fingers having a turn of line around it. He gazed up into the blackness of the sky overhead and saw the thin crescent of moon low down over the hills.

'New moon,' he said. 'It's only a couple of days old. That means spring tides, so we ought to have a real good flow to push us up to Rouen tomorrow. Then in another couple of days we might make Paris.'

'That's great,' Wilbur said. 'When we get there I'm going up the Eiffel Tower – though it's not so high as the Empire State Building back home. That has an elevator up the first sixty or seventy floors, non-stop.'

'I would like to see New York one day,' Michael said slowly. 'I think it must be super. But when we get to Paris I'm going to go out and eat snails before I do anything else. We have a French master at school, and he's always raving about how wonderful Paris is, and all the museums and the places connected with history. You know – Versailles, and the prison of the French Revolution and all that kind of thing. "It makes history live if you know the background," he always says. But I hate trailing round museums and buildings and things. I want to have an exciting time. After all, you can't get snails in England.'

He pulled at his lines to make sure that neither of them had managed to pick up a fish.

'Sure,' Wilbur agreed. 'But the Eiffel Tower is where I'm going first.'

There was silence for a while. Michael was really not

thinking of what he would do in Paris, nor even of the gold bars on the *Marguerite*'s keel. His thoughts had turned back to the previous night and to the great fish which he had so nearly managed to hold on the thin sea-line. He decided that this was a good chance to tell Wilbur the whole story.

'Sounds like a shark for size,' Wilbur said when he came to the end. 'But I guess it couldn't be. Sharks run and pull in jerks. Maybe it was a squid or something, or a big flatfish.'

'It might have been,' Michael agreed. 'It was certainly broad and big.' He was pleased to find that Wilbur believed his story.

'Too bad you lost him,' said Wilbur. 'It would have been good fun to have hauled him aboard. I guess we won't get many big fish up here.'

Michael said he hoped that they would have another night in Le Havre on the way home, and if so he would buy a really heavy tackle and try again. He could perhaps pick up a proper steel hook somewhere, and a steel trace which could not be bitten through. If that were attached to the heaving-line it should be able to hold anything. Even a small whale.

Wilbur interrupted his dreams. 'Are we tied up O.K., Michael? The tide's running up fast, and we're hanging out on the stern rope instead of the bow.'

Michael sat up and looked. The sterns of both craft were projecting into the river at an angle as the water pressed between them and the timbering of the jetty front. The rope from the *Dabchick*'s stern bollard to the top of the jetty looked unpleasantly straight and taut, and although the rope itself was a strong one Michael agreed that the mooring should be made safer. Instead of the two boats being held independently the single stern line of the *Dabchick* was having to hold the weight of both and withstand the force of the tide too.

'I'll go up on the jetty,' he said. 'I'd better take another line over, just to make sure.'

'Looks to me as though we should slack off at the bow,' Wilbur said.

'Yes, that would help. But another stern line would be a good thing anyway. It's at the stern that the tide is working on us.'

'O.K. We've got a good rope on deck. I'll get it.'

'That's fine,' Michael said. 'Give me the noose end, and I'll take it up on to the top of the piles.'

'Still no sign of the big ship,' Wilbur remarked as he put down his fishing-lines and started to disentangle a heap of rope on the deck. 'I hope she comes before we turn in. I'm getting sleepy.'

'Of course she might have gone in by those piles round the bend,' Michael pointed out. 'Or she may not be coming at all.'

At last Wilbur had the rope sorted out and he handed the noose to Michael. 'Had we better tie another on the end? It's not very long,' he said.

'We've got a spare one down below,' Michael replied. 'I'll fetch it, and we can knot them end to end.'

He stood up, crossed to the *Dabchick* and disappeared down the companion ladder, stepping softly so as not to awaken Peter and Jill. Creeping very quietly through into the after cabin he opened a locker under his bunk and began to feel about in the dark for the spare rope which he knew was stowed there. He soon found the coil and drew it out silently. He was just closing the locker when he heard a thud on the forward end of the boat and Wilbur's voice calling urgently from the top of the ladder.

'Michael. Michael. Quick!'

''Sh! You'll wake everybody up,' whispered Michael loudly as he scrambled through with the rope.

But Wilbur hardly dropped his voice. 'Quick! Come up! There's something happening.'

Michael knew from his voice that something was wrong and he raced up on to the deck, heaving the coil of rope up with him.

'Listen!' Wilbur pointed downstream.

A distant noise, swelling louder second by second, came towards them. It was a queer but frightening rumble like that of the thundering of a great waterfall or the torrent running over a dam. It was not a mechanical sound but something ominous, breaking the stillness of the night with a dull relentless roar. The two boys stood motionless, staring out over the dark surface of the water down river as the rushing sound grew continually louder and louder.

Suddenly Michael saw something which made his hair tingle and sent a chill running down between his shoulder blades. He tried to speak, but couldn't. There, only a mere hundred yards away from them, was a great wall of water ploughing up the river, its crest curling white and steep and its edge sweeping the bank.

In the same moment Wilbur saw it too. Leaping on the *Marguerite* he snatched the noose of the spare rope, stumbled back on to the inner boat and across the deck towards the jetty steps.

'Take the other end,' he panted desperately. 'Tie it on anywhere. I'll get the noose on.'

Michael grabbed the rope, hauling it over quickly to find the loose end. The roaring surge of the tidal bore was rushing down upon them but he did not panic. 'Go on, Wilbur, quick! You'll make it!'

At last Michael had the end, but there was no time to run to the *Marguerite*'s stern to tie it on the outer boat. Instead he twisted it twice around the base of one of the *Dabchick*'s stanchions amidships, put the end over, round, and through the loop. There was no time to start making complicated knots.

'I've tied it, Wilbur,' he shouted. 'Get to the top and drop it over a bollard. Hurry up!'

Wilbur was already at the top of the iron ladder, and as he scrambled over the edge on to the jetty Michael put his head through the hatch of the *Dabchick* and shouted for all he was worth.

'Hold on!'

In the next second he flung himself aboard the *Marguerite*, opened the hatch and repeated the warning. 'Hold on tight. Look out!'

But there was no time for those aboard either boat to be more than aware that somebody had awoken them with a shout. The crest of the first wave of the bore was curling above the sterns, and its upward slope pushed them out even more obliquely from the jetty. Michael flung himself flat on the *Marguerite*'s fore-deck beside the hatch and gripped the base of the deck-rail tightly with both hands just as the great wall of water struck.

Up on the jetty Wilbur was feverishly casting round for anything to which he could secure the extra rope. There was no bollard within reach, nothing but the bare planked top of the landing stage. He heard Michael's shout 'Hold on tight!' and as a last resort he threw himself on the planking, pressing the rope as hard as he could over the jetty edge.

Wilbur did not see what happened next, for the little ships were hidden from his view below the edge of the tall jetty. First he heard a splitting crunch, then the fearful sound of smashing crockery as the two craft were rolled nearly on their beams. Finally amid the furious rush of the water came the singing snap as the stern line parted.

It all happened so quickly he had no time even to let go. In a wrench that tore at his wrists and shoulders the line he was still holding was pulled irresistibly over the edge. With a frightened cry Wilbur shot over the edge of the quay and struck the water thirty feet below, just behind the first main wave.

Still holding the rope and smarting painfully where his face had hit the water, Wilbur kicked out furiously for the surface. He was just afloat when the second wave lifted him high in the air and dropped him down again behind it. Once more above the roar of the water he heard a horrible clatter as everything inside the boats was rolled from side to side. Three more lesser waves followed, and then the swell began to even out. More conscious of the fact that he was still alive than of anything else Wilbur now saw that the jetty lay some way behind him and was receding. Desperately he hung on to the noose in the turmoil of the bore.

On board the boats Michael was the only one not taken completely by surprise. Jill had heard his call, but she had done no more than to open her eyes and stare sleepily at the ceiling when something tipped her bunk on its side and flung her violently on to the floor in a mass of bedding. She struggled to her knees just in time for the second wave to throw her across the cabin, and she pitched head first into the mattress of the empty bunk opposite her own.

Peter had sensed danger more quickly. Feeling the curious surge which ran ahead of the wall of the bore he had just swung his legs over the side of his bunk to run on deck and see what was the matter, and when the boat heeled over he half threw himself, half fell on the floor, and the tipping slid him from one side to the other.

The American boat had even less warning. Shirley did not hear Michael's shout at all, and her rude awakening was when the water poured in through the open porthole just above her pillow. Choking and spluttering, she was shot heavily out of bed to be buried in an avalanche of blankets, water, and her own clothes from the rack above, to which were added her suitcase and four drawers from the cupboard as the ship heeled back again.

Mr Tucker was on the starboard side of the ship, up forward, and the first roll forced him against the cabin wall. Reacting quickly he grabbed the outer side of his bunk and succeeded in holding his place. Michael too survived the onslaught of the rushing water through sheer determination not to let go. He buried his head between his outstretched arms and felt the thud as the two boats pounded together, then the wrenching as the light lines which held them side by side snapped like cotton when they heeled.

But he did not lose his head. The moment he felt the swell subsiding he scrambled to his knees and sprawled towards the bows, soaked to the skin. The *Marguerite* was still lunging heavily in the aftermath of the bore, but Michael knew what had to be done. It was imperative that the ship should not be carried on to the rocky shore and smashed.

Steadying himself with legs splayed out sideways he fumbled hastily for the anchor, then suddenly remembered that the Tuckers had lost it in Somme Bay. If only Peter would come up on the *Dabchick* he could fling a line over to hold them.

Mr Tucker staggered on deck in his pyjamas. 'Where's Wilbur?' he asked.

'He's on the jetty,' said Michael. 'He had just run up with another rope. He's safe enough. Is Shirley all right?' he asked.

'She's O.K. A bit shaken maybe, but who isn't?'

Only a few yards away the *Dabchick* was drifting down outside. The lights came on in her cabins and Michael saw Peter scramble quickly through the hatch.

'It's all right, Peter,' he called. 'We're all safe. Throw over the anchor and heave me the end of a rope. You'll find the spare one on deck.'

Peter quickly threw down the kedge, but the new line was nowhere to be seen. It had been tipped overboard. He was just about to go below for another when he heard a cry from somewhere between the boats. Michael heard it too, a wet, gasping splutter more than anything else.

Quickly Michael seized the remains of one of the light lines which had held the boats together.

'It's Wilbur,' he gasped. 'Quick, Peter. Wilbur's somewhere between the boats. Keep them apart. He might be crushed between them.' He called reassuringly towards where he could now make out a splashing close to the *Dabchick*'s side.

'All right, Wilbur. I see you. I'll throw the lifebuoy.'

'I'm O.K. – I think,' gasped Wilbur. 'I've still got the rope.'

'Haul him in, Peter,' Michael shouted. 'It's that rope tied on amidships, below the rail.'

Hurriedly Peter took up the line and drew Wilbur in alongside. Then lying right down on the catwalk he held on with one arm and reached for the boy's hand with the other. At last he had hold of him safely, and when Jill too found her way up on deck over the wreckage strewn about inside the boat, she helped her brother to haul Wilbur aboard.

'Take him below, Jill. I'll see that we're tied up to the others again.' Peter went back to the bows to recover what was left of the bow rope, and heaved the end across to Mr Tucker. The *Marguerite* swung, and began to straighten up a short way astern.

Jill, pale with the shock of what had happened, took Wilbur down below. He was shivering in his wet clothes and she picked up a blanket from among the debris. 'Here, take this, and get your wet things off,' she said, trying to sound calm.

'I'm sorry,' he spluttered. 'I tried to hold them, but I couldn't.'

'I shouldn't think anything could have held us in that,' said Jill. 'What on earth happened?'

'I think I know,' he said with a shiver. He struggled to undo his tie, but his fingers were numb with the strain of holding the rope.

'Here,' said Jill, 'I'll do it.' She worked at the knot, and suddenly Wilbur laughed.

'You wouldn't have a French dictionary aboard?' he asked.

'Yes, in the drawer.' Jill freed his tie and began to help him off with his shirt. 'Why do you want a dictionary?'

'I can manage my clothes,' Wilbur said. 'You have a look-see in the dictionary.'

Still puzzled, Jill rummaged in a drawer and brought out the book. Wilbur drew off his dripping shirt and dumped it on the floor.

'Have a look-see at what it says under "mascaret",' he repeated as he pulled the blanket over his shoulders. 'Go on, I want to know.'

Jill turned the pages until she found the place.

'Mascaret, noun, masculine,' she read out slowly, peering at the small print in the dim light. 'Tidal wave. Especially the great bore on the River Seine which reaches a height of several feet.'

Wilbur laughed. 'That's what I thought. I guess there's a moral to this, Jill. If you don't understand what people are saying – well, it's kind of sensible to find out before it's too late.'

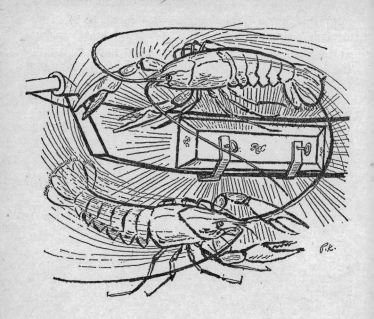

7. Discovery at the Lock

By drawing the two craft together Michael was able to get back aboard the *Dabchick* again, and he went below to help Peter and Jill clear up the mess. Bedclothes were on the floor, the table was overturned, and the galley was running with a mixture of methylated spirit and orange squash in which lumps of sugar melted forlornly away. The eggs had been tipped out of the rack on to the floor, but Jill managed to salvage most of them and slop the yolks and whites into a pan.

'It's your turn to cook tomorrow, Michael,' she said, trying to sound cheerful although she was nearly crying. 'You always like to make scrambled eggs, and there's enough here for days.'

'Well, it's better than losing them altogether,' said Michael, carefully picking up some of the broken glass and dropping it in a bucket. 'And if you ask me, we're lucky it was no worse. If we had been tied round the side of that jetty we should have been smashed to smithereens.'

Jill was busy putting the pans back again on their shelf when she stumbled suddenly forward and hit her head on the sink as the *Dabchick* heaved and lurched. She gave a little cry, more of fright than of pain, fearing instinctively that another bore was running down upon them. Peter stepped up the ladder and looked out.

'It's all right,' he reassured the others. 'It's a big ship running down river.'

Michael ran to a porthole and stared out at the great white side of a cargo liner gliding by, the lights shining bright in her portholes and at her mastheads.

'She's huge,' he exclaimed, steadying himself as their own little ship rocked on the wash. 'Seven or eight thousand tons, any day.'

'I think we should move,' Peter said as he returned below. 'I don't like hanging at anchor in this colossal tide with these big fellows belting down the river. There are a couple more in sight, and just here we're right on the outside of the bend. They're cutting in fairly fine past us to take the deep water.'

Jill stood up. 'Do you think it's safe to go on in the dark, Peter?' She sounded anxious.

'Oh, it's safe enough,' Peter answered. 'If you look out you'll see there are red and green lights on the banks all the way up. It's a lot safer than staying here, and we don't need to go fast. So long as we run up slowly the tide can do most of the work.'

He stepped over to the *Marguerite* again and put his head through the hatch. 'Hello, there,' he called. 'We think we should go on up river. There are ships coming down this side, and we'll have no peace all night.'

'O.K. I'm game,' said the American, emerging from the galley with a basinful of broken china. 'Anything you say.'

'How's Wilbur?' Peter asked.

'I'm fine,' came a voice from the fore-cabin. 'And if we're getting going then I'm getting out of bed again.' And with a thud he swung over the side of his bunk and appeared grinning in the doorway.

'Then let's get under way,' Peter said. 'I've got a good chart of the river and we can lead ahead.'

After waiting to let the two big ships pass, Peter started up the engine and moved the *Dabchick* up on her anchor, hovering and swaying in the swirling tide whilst Jill and Michael hauled in the chain. At last the anchor broke surface and Michael waved his hand. The two craft were let go from each other and Peter looked behind to make sure that nothing was coming, then slid round to port and into the middle of the great river. By the time he had straightened up, the *Marguerite* was swinging away to follow him.

Jill came back to the wheelhouse but Michael went below to finish tidying up.

'I know Daddy always says crooks don't behave like crooks,' Jill said slowly. 'But I don't believe the Tuckers are crooks. Really I don't.'

'Oh, don't you? And why not?'

'I don't really know,' Jill admitted. 'I just feel that way about them, that's all. And besides, there's something else. Daddy always says that crooks are cowardly, but you can't say Wilbur was cowardly. He tried to get the boats held with another line at the very last moment, and he never complained at all about being thrown in the river, right off the very top of that enormous high landing-stage.'

'That's true,' Peter agreed. 'But then Wilbur may not know anything about what his father does. Nor may Shirley if it comes to that, and as a matter of fact I don't think she does.'

'Then there's no reason why we shouldn't make real friends with them,' Jill said.

'It ought to help us.'

'No, not like that. I mean real friends of our own, not just as a means to finding out about the bullion.'

Peter considered. 'Well, perhaps. Though I don't know that they'll be friends with us after Dad has had their father arrested when we get to Paris.'

'If he's really a crook,' Jill said. 'I don't think he is.'

'You did before.'

'Yes, I know. Only now I just don't think he is, somehow.'

Peter laughed. 'Take hold of yourself,' he said. 'You're slipping. If he isn't a crook why has he got those bars of the Chesterfield gold stuck on his keel?'

'I don't know. Perhaps he doesn't know they're there.'

'Honestly you're going soft,' said Peter. 'Anybody who's in a boat with stolen bullion on the keel must jolly well know it's there, and if he knows it's there he's a crook all right, even if his job is only to deliver it. It stands to reason.'

'I know it stands to reason, but I still don't think it's true. And I'll tell you another thing.'

'Go on, then.'

'Crooks are selfish, always. But Mr Tucker took us out on that binge in Dieppe.'

'Well, dash it all,' said Peter. 'We had saved them from a pretty nasty mess-up in Somme Bay. He was grateful, that's all.'

'That's just the point. Daddy says crooks are never grateful, not for anything. They even doublecross their own friends all the time.'

'Perhaps they do, but that's no reason why they couldn't feel generous to people who help them. They must have ordinary decent feelings.'

But Jill shook her head. 'They can't have, Peter, or they wouldn't be crooks. And in this case surely Mr Tucker wouldn't be involved in pinching the gold that was going to provide a children's hospital and at the same time take us out to dinner when he needn't have done so. The one thing is mean, the other isn't. It just doesn't make sense.'

'All right then, it doesn't,' said Peter irritably. 'But I

would like to see you tell the French police and Dad when they come to arrest him that Mr Tucker is not involved in the robbery. Perhaps you can explain how the gold came to be on their boat.'

'Perhaps somebody put it there without their knowing.'

'And somebody else is going to take it off again without their knowing, I suppose.'

'I don't see why not.'

'Well, I do.'

When the daylight began to break Peter opened up the engine still further. Soon afterwards he turned off the navigation lights. Jill and Michael had long since dropped off to sleep in the corners of the wheelhouse and Peter decided to let them doze on. Though his eyes had been tired with staring ahead in the dark, the growing daylight made things easier, and he felt surprisingly fresh as he stood at the wheel for the fifth hour in succession. Looking round, he saw that the *Marguerite* was still following, holding her position a couple of hundred yards astern.

Seven o'clock brought the *Dabchick* in past the lower dock area of Rouen on the starboard side, whilst on the opposite shore the cliffs rose high, densely covered in beeches. The ebb was beginning to tell now, so Peter cut close inshore for slacker water and sidled past the big ships anchored in the river roadsteads or lying off the wharves. Swedes, Danes, a Panamanian tanker, Dutchmen, a Finn unloading timber, a couple of British coasters, a big passenger liner, the river was full of magnificent great ships. Knowing Michael would be sorry to miss the sight, Peter shook him gently.

'Nearly at Rouen, Michael.'

Michael stood up, stretched, and blinked. 'Gosh! Just look at all those super ships. I'm glad you woke me up.'

'There's Rouen.' Peter pointed ahead to where the great towers and slim central spire of the cathedral rose dimly above the town in the morning haze.

The main quays were now in view on the port side and

cranes were swinging their loads out from the lines of railway wagons to drop them in the holds. A series of bridges
lay at the end of a straight reach, but just before them was
a stone embankment against which a varied collection of
craft were tied, a pile driver, a dredger, a tangle of lighters
and tugs. There was a hundred feet or more of unoccupied
quay and Peter drew over, eased down, and allowed the
current to slide the *Dabchick* gently up to the wall. This was
Rouen, and Rouen meant breakfast. Altogether he was not
at all sorry.

If Peter had expected just to have breakfast at Rouen, he
had expected too little. Everybody seemed happy to wander
about the town afterwards, sauntering through the streets of
beautiful old houses still left after the bombardment of 1945,
watching the flower-sellers under their coloured umbrellas,
and staring in open-eyed wonder at the market with its
hundreds of different local cheeses. The morning slipped
away and the two crews had lunch together on shore in
spite of Peter's misgivings about leaving the *Marguerite* unwatched.

'Well, I suppose we might as well move on up river,' Peter
said, as they left the café. He liked being abroad, and
he would willingly have spent all day wandering round
the narrow streets of the old city, but it was much more
important to escort the *Marguerite* up to Paris without
delay.

'Plenty of time, plenty of time,' said Mr Tucker. 'I guess
we might take another look around in the market. It's kind
of picturesque, don't you think so?'

'It's lovely,' Jill said.

'Then let's stay a while,' said the American. 'No point in
being in a hurry on vacation. What do you say, Shirley?'

Shirley agreed at once. They hadn't seen half of what
there must be to see, she said.

So in spite of the misgivings of Peter and his crew, and of
Wilbur too – who just preferred being under way to trailing
round the shops and streets – they returned once more to

the rows of stalls of cheese and butter, cloth and flowers, meat and cheap toys and mountains of fruit.

The market certainly was attractive, but after another twenty minutes they had been through it from end to end. Mr Tucker, however, was still not ready to leave the town. He insisted on taking the two girls into one shop after another until he found a blouse for Shirley and a pretty little en- amelled brooch for Jill. The boys waited outside on the pave- ment, not envious but wanting to get back aboard. Peter was becoming impatient to get under way again, but he could hardly say so, particularly when Mr Tucker was buy- ing his presents.

The time slipped by. The afternoon was nearly gone, and it was not until a quarter to four that the two boats headed up river again with a fair tide behind their sterns, the *Dabchick* still leading.

There were many islands in the river here, but otherwise it was not very spectacular. Michael was now at the wheel of the *Dabchick* and he put on a good turn of speed, but even so it was just on seven o'clock before the first of the great locks came into view round a bend. There were three locks side by side, and a coaster and a string of barges were just coming out of the left-hand pen.

Peter was turning the pages of the chart. 'That's where we are,' he said. 'Ecluse – that's a lock – de Poses. Two hundred and two kilometres from Paris. Let's see, that's about a hundred and twenty-six miles.'

'It looks as though we're in luck with the lock,' Michael said. 'As soon as those ships are out we can have the whole thing to ourselves.'

Wilbur was keeping the *Marguerite* well back, two or three hundred yards behind the *Dabchick*, to give the outcoming craft plenty of room to manoeuvre. As soon as the last of the barges was clear, Michael went ahead into the lock, but Wilbur waited to let the coaster run down past him. She was the *Marne*, a British ship, and the crew coiling the hawsers on the fore-deck waved to him in a friendly fashion as they passed close by. Then came the barges, and at last Wilbur began to move up on the lock.

The *Dabchick* was already inside and the *Marguerite* no more than a hundred yards away when the signal light changed from green to red and the great gates started to close.

'Well, of all the idiotic things to do,' Michael exclaimed as he saw the gates begin to swing. 'They're shutting them out.'

Jill was already on the quayside with the ropes. 'Tell them not to shut the gates,' Peter called up to her. 'Tell the chap the *Marguerite* is just coming in.'

'I'll try.' Jill dropped the nooses over the bollards and ran up to the control cabin where the engineer was sitting back in his chair beside a row of push buttons.

'Monsieur . . .'

'Mademoiselle?'

'Monsieur, il y a un autre bateau là.' She pointed down beyond the lock, and at the same moment Wilbur gave a long toot on the hooter.

As the gates closed with a clang the engineer took his finger off the button marked *fermer*. He pressed another to operate the sluices which filled the lock, and then looked at Jill and shook his head.

'Sept heures – finis,' he said. And he pointed at the clock on the lock-house opposite. He tapped his watch too, just to rub it in. The time was about one and a half minutes after seven.

'Finis?'

'Oui. On peut passer demain à six heures.'

'Demain! Not till tomorrow?' Jill's French began to collapse in her annoyance.

'Oui, demain.' He changed the subject. 'Vous allez à Paris?'

'Oui.'

The lock-keeper pointed out of the window upstream. They could lie up against the bank on the bend, he said.

E

They would not be disturbed during the night. Then their friends could join them in the morning.

The lock was filling rapidly and Jill returned to the boat.

'No luck,' she said. 'Not till tomorrow. They shut at seven apparently.'

'But honestly it's a bit thick,' Michael said. 'Wilbur would have been inside in less than half a minute.'

The upper gates began to swing back. Jill and Peter flicked off the ropes and Michael ran slowly out into the reach above.

'There's something funny about this business,' said Peter. 'I don't like it. I think it was all arranged.'

'Arranged? What do you mean?' Jill asked.

'Well, if the Tuckers wanted to give us the slip this is a good way to do it. They could be back at Le Havre before we could get down through the lock again to run after them. I shouldn't be a bit surprised if they're going to turn back. Either that, or they're going to unload the gold here. It certainly looked as though they hung back on purpose to let us get in by ourselves.'

'But how could they know?'

'Easily. Don't forget they may have done this trip before. They probably knew the lock closed at seven. And it was they who took so long wandering round Rouen that we didn't leave till late afternoon. If you ask me they planned the thing pretty cleverly, arriving here just in time to be cut off from us.'

'They couldn't have planned it to the minute, surely,' Jill objected.

'Well, they did,' Michael said. 'And for all we know the chap at the lock is an accomplice.'

'But they haven't had a chance to speak to him.'

'No need to,' said Peter. 'The way they hung back made it pretty obvious what they wanted him to do.'

'That might have been a message to him which Mr Tucker handed in at Tancarville,' Jill said.

'It probably was,' Peter agreed. 'Anyway, they've certainly given us the slip right enough. We'll have to watch them all night again.'

Jill sighed. 'It seems as though we're never going to get a night's sleep,' she said.

'What are we going to do if they turn back?' Michael asked.

'We should have to tell the police, I suppose,' Peter said.

'I shouldn't think there's a policeman for miles.'

'There must be a phone at the lock,' Jill said.

'That's not a lot of use,' said Michael. 'Not if the lock-keeper is in league with them.'

'Well, let's leave that until we see what happens,' Peter said.

They moored up quickly and Peter ran back down the tow-path towards the lock to see what was happening, but as soon as the lower river came into view he was relieved to see that the *Marguerite* was just in process of tying up. Below the lock a high spit projected downstream between the lock approach and the big weir pool, and on the one side it was flanked by a long range of mooring piles. The *Marguerite* lay beside them, and Shirley was climbing a ladder to the top of the piles, carrying the lines.

Peter ran across the locks. 'I'm sorry we got in and you didn't,' he said as he reached the top of the piles beside Shirley.

'I think they're crazy,' she said with a laugh. 'But it can't be helped. We'll just have to wait.'

Peter was still wondering what Mr Tucker's intentions were. 'Anyway, we can have the evening together,' he said with a sudden inspiration. 'You'll all come to supper on the *Dabchick* in half an hour. How's that?'

'Fine, Peter. I'll go down and tell the others, then I'll come right over and give Jill a hand with the cooking.'

Back at the *Dabchick* again Peter held a hurried consultation with his crew. On the whole they were not inclined to think that the *Marguerite* would really give them the slip during the night, because it would look very suspicious. But there was always the chance that the American could phone up an accomplice and have him come and collect the gold before dawn. Poses was a deserted spot right out in the country, and nothing could be easier. The *Marguerite* would have to be kept under close observation all night long.

'But we can't see her at all from here,' Jill said.

'I know. We'll just have to take it in turns to hide somewhere close to where she is, and run watches again,' Peter said.

Before long Shirley arrived and she and Jill got busy making the supper while Michael laid the table and Peter tidied the saloon. The other guests were not long in coming and the combined companies made the most of an excellent meal, the main course of which had to be omelet to use up the broken eggs. But it was a bacon omelet made by Shirley, and they all congratulated her on a very fine piece of work.

Lack of sleep soon brought yawns all round, and at nine o'clock the *Marguerite* party decided it was time to say good night. The others gave them ten minutes to get clear and then Jill was to take the first watch. Peter walked down towards the locks with her, but instead of crossing to the spit they went down the path on the opposite side, where it was partly hidden from the river by a thin line of scrub trees. Almost straight across from the *Marguerite* Peter found a good position for Jill in some soft long grass among the bushes.

'Here, take this,' he said, giving her his jacket. 'And I'll just slip back for a rug.'

But Jill insisted that she would not need one. The night was soft and warm, and there was no breeze at all. She would be much more likely to drop off to sleep, she said, if she were given too much of a bed.

Peter was just going to leave her, when he considered their situation. Here they were, right out in the wilds with only the lock cottages anywhere near, and at least a suspicion that there might be serious business ahead. He did not care to leave his sister alone in the dark under such circumstances.

'Jill,' he said quietly, 'I'm going to stay.'

'Nonsense,' she whispered. 'I can manage.'

'Yes, I know. But . . . well, I would rather.'

'But you had no sleep at all last night,' she objected. 'I'll be all right, really I will.'

'All the same, I'm staying too. Only I'll just run back and tell Michael in case he wonders where I am.'

By the time that the lights went out aboard the *Marguerite* Peter and Jill were settling down comfortably to watch. Peter had brought back a couple of blankets, and before midnight Jill had dozed off. He decided there was no point in waking her unless something happened. From time to time he raised his head and looked across through the bushes, but all was quiet. It was after two o'clock in the morning that he distinctly heard a heavy bump from across the water.

Instantly he was alert. As the lights went on in the *Marguerite*'s saloon he gently squeezed Jill's hand and woke her.

'Don't make a sound,' he whispered. 'Something's going on. Look.'

Jill sat up quickly and rubbed her eyes.

The hatch of the boat slid open with a sharp click, and in the flood of light from inside the saloon Peter and Jill saw Wilbur's head appear. Then he came on deck, looked around, and called loudly down the hatchway. In the stillness of the night it was easy to hear his words.

'Pop, quick,' he called. 'The water has dropped. We're heeling over. Come up, quick!'

'Gosh, he's right,' Peter whispered. 'Look, she's got a terrific list on. The thump I heard was probably poor old Wilbur falling out of his bunk.'

The details of what happened were not easily seen from across the river. Mr Tucker and Shirley both heard Wilbur's shout, and scrambling up on deck they saw that the boat was already too far for there to be any chance of pulling her upright again.

But at least it was possible to prevent her from falling right over on her side if the water should drop any farther. Working as fast as possible the American put a double line across from the outer rail, round one of the piles and back again, whilst Wilbur searched below for every available piece of rope. He then put one of the dinghy oars through between the two sets of lines and with Shirley's help he managed gradually to force it round and round and round, over and over, to twist up the ropes windlass-fashion until they were as tight as steel hawsers. He then held the oar firmly while Shirley lashed the end of it to the rail to prevent it from spinning back.

With the ropes Wilbur had collected, the same thing was done a second time, nearer to the stern. Peter and Jill heard Mr Tucker advise the others not to move unnecessarily about the boat, and in any case to keep to the inward side of the ship.

The next thing they heard was alarming. 'Do you think we're O.K., Pop?' Shirley called. 'How do you say I go fetch Peter and see what he thinks?'

'If anybody starts up the ladder, we must move and quickly too,' Peter whispered to his sister. 'We can't have them finding we're not aboard our own boat.'

But Mr Tucker's answer was a relief. 'We're fine. Let them sleep. There's nothing Peter could do,' he said. 'We can turn in again.'

'I'll stay on deck,' said Wilbur. 'I'm not sleepy any more. I'll keep a watch on things.'

'O.K.' Mr Tucker inspected the twisted ropes once more and went below with Shirley. A few minutes later the boat was again in darkness and Peter and Jill lay down once more. Soon, without meaning to, they had both fallen asleep.

Wilbur sat on deck in the warm night air. He had only his pyjamas on, but he did not feel at all cold, and after a while he took the flash-lamp from the wheelhouse and shone it down over the side between the boat and the piles. There was certainly not much water. The loose rocks and stones of the river bottom were breaking surface near the edge.

He tiptoed gently along the catwalk, creeping under the taut ropes, and shone his light downwards once more, this time nearer the stern. Here there was no more than fifteen inches of water alongside. He was not at all sure that the level was not still falling and so he shone the beam of the torch on a stone which was just awash, and tried to make out whether it was slowly emerging from the surface or not.

Suddenly something caught his eye. He was absolutely certain that he saw a curious object protrude for a moment from under the edge of the stone, but before he really had a chance to see what it was it disappeared again. He knelt on the catwalk and peered down at the stone, moving the beam of light to shine fully on its edge.

For nearly a minute nothing happened and Wilbur had almost given up hope when once again the shape appeared. It consisted of two greenish-brown little arms, curved in towards each other and ending in pincer claws. Between them were two tiny eyes on short stalks, and a pair of great long whiskers.

As Wilbur stared in astonishment the creature came right out from under the stone. It was four or five inches long, and its body ended in a sort of fringed fan. At first the animal moved on its legs and then it plunged ahead with a fluttering swimming motion and disappeared under the boat.

'Baby lobster,' said Wilbur almost aloud. And then, 'But it can't be. Not up here, in fresh water. Lobsters live in the sea.'

Then he had an idea. Tiptoeing softly to the hatch as though afraid to frighten the strange animal he went below and returned with the salad-strainer from the galley, and the string bag which Shirley used for the household shopping, Then he rolled up his pyjama trousers and lowered himself cautiously over the stern. The bottom was rough and stony.

but the water did not come up to his knees and it was wonderfully warm.

Very gingerly he crept in between the hull and the piles. There was room enough for him now that the boat was leaning right out, and holding the lamp and the strainer and bag in one hand he bent down and cautiously turned over a stone with no result.

He tried another, and then another, and at the fourth stone he saw one of the queer creatures. It sat quite still in the beam of the lamp, twiddling its whiskers.

Wilbur had not enough hands, so he stuck the string bag in the belt of his pyjama trousers and just managed to hold the flash-lamp in his teeth. Then very cautiously he opened the strainer and lowered it into the water, facing the animal and about a foot in front of it. When all was ready he put his other hand behind the animal and touched its fan-shaped hind-end.

The creature jumped forward, straight into the strainer, and Wilbur quickly scooped it out of the water to examine it. Its pincers were snapping with little clicks and there was no doubt that it was very much like a small lobster.

'And if it's a kind of lobster it ought to be good eats,' he whispered to himself. So he took up the string bag, tipped the creature in, and hanging the bag on a bolt of the piling he resumed his hunt.

The second one escaped before he had time to lift out the strainer, but before long he had two more, one of which he saw just creeping over the stones. With three now in his bag he called a halt and decided to fetch Michael. If Michael came to help it would be much easier.

The very first tinge of grey light was just beginning to break the darkness. Climbing back on board, Wilbur found that he could not now reach even the bottom rung of the shore ladder, so he lowered the dinghy gently on the outer side, and, without bothering to put on anything more except a pair of shoes, he climbed aboard it. Both the oars were in use in his father's improvised windlasses, but Wilbur managed

to paddle the boat across with one of the floorboards until
he reached the opposite bank, where the grass sloped down
to the stony foreshore. Careful not to run the dinghy on the
rocks, he slipped over the side and paddled towards the
shore with his shoes hung round his neck.

It was the splashing which woke Peter this time. Sitting
up straight he saw to his horror that Wilbur was just tying
the painter of the dinghy round a big stone at the foot of the
bank not a dozen yards away. It was too late to escape.
Whatever Wilbur was up to, he could not possibly reach the
top of the bank without discovering them. Quickly deciding
that the only thing to do was to reveal their presence before
Wilbur could stumble on them by accident, he gripped Jill's
arm and pulled her into a sitting position and at the same
time called out.

'Hello there, Wilbur.'

'Peter! Gee, you made me jump.'

Peter stood up, and so did Jill, yawning.

'We couldn't sleep aboard,' said Peter. 'Too hot and
stuffy. So Jill and I got up early and er . . . came down here
where it's cool.'

'Hello, Wilbur,' said Jill as Peter nudged her.

Wilbur seemed to accept their being there as quite natural.
'Come and have a look-see,' he said excitedly, shining his
flash-lamp into the dinghy. 'Come on.'

Jill and Peter stepped down to the edge of the water.

'Why, whatever are those?' Jill asked, staring at the
strange animals.

'They must be crayfish,' said Peter.

'Crawfish are pink,' Wilbur said.

'Only when they're cooked I expect. All those crab and
lobster things go pink on boiling,' Jill explained.

'I'm certain they're crayfish,' Peter decided. 'They
couldn't be anything else.'

'That's fine,' Wilbur exclaimed. 'Crawfish are good to
eat, too. We had a big dish of them back home when Pop
had some folks in to dinner.'

Jill wondered how on earth Wilbur had managed to catch them, and she and Peter laughed when he showed them the salad-strainer and explained. 'I was rowing over to get Michael,' he added. 'He wouldn't like to miss a bit of fishing.'

'Good idea,' agreed Peter.

'Only I couldn't use the oars,' Wilbur continued. He explained in detail about the *Marguerite* having been dropped by the tide, and Jill and Peter appeared to listen attentively, just as though they had not seen the incident for themselves already.

'Jill, you run back and send Michael along,' Peter said when Wilbur had finished. 'And you might as well try to get to sleep on board again now that it's cooler. I'll stay here with Wilbur until he comes.'

'And tell him to bring something to help catch crawfish in,' called Wilbur as Jill went off along the path, carrying the blankets.

'Right, I will.'

As soon as Jill gently woke him with a tale of queer creatures to be caught, Michael was wide awake in a moment. He slipped out of his bunk and put on his shorts. Taking with him a pail to hold the catch he ran speedily down to the lock where Peter and Wilbur were waiting for him. Soon they were all three gliding across to the opposite shore to get to work again.

Michael and Wilbur got out and began to creep among the rocks whilst Peter hovered beside them in the dinghy so that they could keep their pail in it and use it as a depot ship for their activities.

Michael had never seen crayfish before and he was tremendously excited. The crayfish were most obliging too, and in the increasing daylight Wilbur managed now and then to see the little heads poking out from between the piling as well as under the edges of the rocks. Michael did not fancy tackling them with his bare hands except to tickle them from behind, but Wilbur managed several times to snatch one up in his fingers and drop it in the pail before it had time to pinch him with its claws. There were eels too lurking among the piles, but they were only small ones, and, in any case, they were far too elusive to catch by hand. Michael succeeded in driving one into the strainer but it was small enough to squeeze out through the mesh again.

'It wasn't much more than a shoe-lace,' said Wilbur. 'Let's forget the eels and take the crawfish.'

With a haul of fifteen crayfish down to the end of the point, the boys decided to move up ahead of the *Marguerite* and search the stretch up towards the lock.

'We need plenty more if we can catch them,' Wilbur said. 'Half a dozen apiece if we can, to make a real feed.'

So they climbed into the dinghy and Peter began to paddle them up.

'That could have been nasty,' said Michael with a nod towards the *Marguerite*. 'She might have gone right over. Honestly, they are donkeys to put down these mooring piles where the river dries right out.'

'I guess we might have known,' said Wilbur. 'We knew it was tidal and we could easily have sounded.'

The water was now at its lowest ebb, and as they came level with the stern of the boat Michael suddenly realized that the *Marguerite*'s keel was out of the water. And if the keel was visible something else should be visible too.

Wilbur was leaning over the bow of the dinghy peering down for signs of prey, so Michael leaned forward and whispered in Peter's ear.

'The gold! We shall be able to see it!'

Peter turned his head quickly to look underneath the hull, and Michael too stared at the long, shallow keel as it came into view. There it was, clear and clean with its copper-red anti-fouling paint, and they could see the whole length of it. But there was no sign of any gold, nor of the clamps which Jill had said were there.

Peter and Michael exchanged curious glances, then looked once more. There was no doubt about it; the *Marguerite*'s secret cargo had gone, and only the chipped paint showed where the bars had been tightly squeezed against the keel.

'Wilbur,' Peter said suddenly, trying to make his voice sound natural. 'Michael and I have just got to go back to the *Dabchick* for a few minutes to see to the engine. It needs a check over before we go on up to Paris. We'll leave you here with your dinghy. I'll just row up to the ladder by the lock gates, and we'll climb ashore.'

'Couldn't you fix the engine later?' Wilbur sounded rather disappointed.

'Well . . . er . . . I think we had better see to it now,' Peter answered. 'We don't want to delay you later.'

'We won't be long,' added Michael. 'We'll come back as soon as we can.' And he really hoped so, because he was enjoying hunting for crayfish.

'O.K. then. But hurry back. It's a lot easier catching craw-fish with two.'

Peter rowed the dinghy up to the ladder, and Michael and he set off quickly across the lock-gates.

'Well, what do you make of it?' Peter whispered as they went.

'I suppose Jill couldn't have made a mistake . . .'

'No. She said she saw the monogram stamped on the bars.'

Michael considered. 'Perhaps the gold just came adrift. They might have touched bottom somewhere and knocked it off.'

'It's possible – but I don't think so, and I'll tell you why. When Wilbur found the boat was being left high and dry and woke the others, his father's first concern would have been to see that the gold was not visible. He would have gone over the side to look. But he didn't. He just braced up the boat with lines and turned in again. Besides, how about Wilbur? If he knew the gold was on the keel and suddenly found it had gone he would have found some excuse to get back aboard and tell his father. And if he didn't know there was gold on the keel Mr Tucker would never have let him go messing about around the hull where he might easily see it. No, Mr Tucker must have known very well that the gold had gone. Which means that it must already have been handed over.'

'But he couldn't have delivered it without our knowing,' Michael objected as they broke into a run. 'Let's see what Jill thinks.'

Back on board there was an earnest meeting in Jill's cabin. Peter told her the news as she sat up in her bunk. She listened carefully and agreed with Peter that Mr Tucker must have known that it was safe to let the bottom of the *Marguerite* be seen when the tide left her high and dry. But she too was puzzled.

'Let's go over the last few days and remember what happened,' she said with practical sense. 'We might see when they could have delivered the cargo, and where.'

'Good idea,' Michael agreed. 'Here goes. Tuesday we find them stuck in Somme Bay and you dive down and see the gold.'

'Right,' said Peter. 'Then we went to Dieppe and had them under observation all night.'

'Ditto at Le Havre,' said Michael. 'Then we fuelled and ran through the canal, and moored up for the night by that refinery. That was Wednesday.'

'Then we were knocked about by the bore,' Jill continued. 'I suppose it couldn't have come off in all that rocking?'

'We never hit the bottom, nor did they,' Peter pointed out. 'Besides, there must have been plenty of water, because tankers berth there.'

'Anyway we're agreed it couldn't have been lost by accident,' Michael said. 'Otherwise Mr Tucker would have had the wind up this morning.'

'Yes, I forgot that,' Jill said.

'Well, Thursday breakfast-time we were at Rouen. We left the *Marguerite* unguarded, but we never lost sight of the Tuckers all day. Besides, nobody could have tampered with the boat at that quay in the centre of the town. Not in broad daylight anyway.'

'All right, then, they couldn't,' said Michael. 'But in that case I don't see that we're getting anywhere. After Rouen we came straight up here, and the gold was gone by this morning. I suppose you two are quite sure nothing happened during the night? After all, it was a bit fishy the way they managed to get left out of the lock yesterday evening. You thought so too.'

Peter shook his head. 'I know. But I was awake the whole time until Wilbur roused them because the boat was listing. There was no funny business in the dark, I can swear to that.'

'Then all we've worked out is that they couldn't have got rid of the gold,' Michael said. 'But they have done, and what's more, they know they have done. It looks to me as though getting shut out of the lock last night was really an accident and they unshipped the stuff at Rouen.'

'How?' Peter asked.

'I don't know how. But somebody might have done it while we were all away in the town. That fits in with the way the Tuckers kept dawdling about in the shops and the market. They were keeping us out of the way.'

'And my brooch,' said Jill. 'I suppose that was only to take up time, too.' She looked down rather sadly at where it was pinned in her blouse. 'It's a lovely one, and I thought he was buying it for me as a real present, not just to keep us out of the way. I don't think I like it any more.' And she began to unfasten it.

'Don't be silly,' Michael said. 'If you like it, what does it matter? Some people would be glad to have something given them by a famous crook. He's probably a Chicago gangster, which makes the brooch much more interesting.'

'We can't discuss that now,' said Peter. 'The thing is, what are we to do now?'

Jill stood up. 'I really think we ought to try to phone Daddy in Paris and tell him what has happened,' she said decidedly. 'We can stop somewhere during the morning and telephone.'

'I don't see what Dad can do about it,' Peter objected.

'We know the gold has gone, and we can tell him about that when we get there. We might make the outskirts by tonight if we get cracking as soon as the lock opens to let the *Marguerite* up. . . .'

He was cut short by a knock on the porthole glass. Wilbur was peering in from the tow-path, a broad grin on his face. With presence of mind Jill waved to him. 'Hello, Wilbur,' she called. 'Any luck with the fishing?'

Wilbur jumped on to the boat and soon he was coming down the ladder. 'There's no crawfish just around the lock,' he said. 'I thought maybe I could look along by the bank up here, and then, when Michael was finished helping Peter to get the engine fixed, he could come too.'

Peter realized that it hardly looked as though they had been working as engineers. Their hands were much too clean.

'We've nothing more to do, really,' he said. 'The engine's all fixed ready to go. You and Michael can carry on with your hunting. Jill and I might as well be getting the cabins straight. It will be breakfast-time before long.'

The two boys jumped ashore. The water above the lock was perfectly still, with here and there a faint wisp of mist drifting over it like steam, but the sun was really up at last, at the bottom of a clear blue sky. Shining obliquely on the water it lit up the bank where the stones fell away below the surface. Wilbur moved cautiously along the rocky edge with Michael behind him.

Suddenly he pointed. 'Crawfish. Quick, give me the strainer.' And he bent down slowly with the open trap in his hand.

The crayfish was a beauty. He sat in a wide cleft, twiddling his feelers and staring with his stalky eyes at Wilbur. As the strainer came closer, his whiskers stopped, motionless.

'Tickle him from behind, Michael,' Wilbur whispered.

Very slowly Michael reached down through the water towards the creature, which opened and shut its handsome pincers as though wondering whether to give the pink fingers a sharp nip. Still Michael's hand drew nearer, but at the last moment the crayfish jumped out of the crevice and darted along the side of the bank.

'After him!' Michael cried. And they stumbled forward through the water.

Two or three yards farther ahead the crayfish settled gently on a stone. Wilbur tried to imprison it with the strainer, but once more the creature shot clear and swam busily with his tail fan into the space between the *Dabchick*'s stern and the bank.

'I know what,' Michael said, clambering hurriedly out on to the bank. 'I'll slacken off the stern rope so we can get in after him.'

He eased the rope from round a tree and pushed on the side of the boat to swing it slowly away from the bank. Then he lay on the grass and peered over the edge of the piling into the water.

'I can't see him,' Wilbur said, disappointed. 'Either he's gone away between the piles, or he's moved out under the boat into deep water. Or he might be in the shadow of the boat.'

Michael jumped up again and fetched the flashlight which was lying beside the bucket. 'I'll sweep the bottom with this,' he suggested. 'Then if he's there we ought to be able to see him.'

Wilbur put his face right close against the water as Michael probed among the stones with the sharp beam of the light. The crayfish seemed to have disappeared but suddenly Wilbur let out a sharp exclamation.

'Hey, just shine back there, Michael. Down there, below the hull. I thought I saw something.'

Michael obliged, and switched the beam to below the planking. When suddenly the light was reflected bright and golden from somewhere just ahead of the *Dabchick*'s propeller he was so completely taken by surprise that he allowed the beam to linger on the spot for a moment or two before he switched it off.

'What's that under the boat?' Wilbur asked directly.

'I . . . I don't know,' Michael said rather lamely.

'Here, give me that flash.' Wilbur almost snatched it from him. 'We'll have a look-see,' he declared. 'This flash is O.K. for under water.' And he held it as far under the boat as he could before pressing the button.

'Gold,' he exclaimed in wonder. 'Gold! Great bars of it!'

'It can't be,' Michael said, desperately trying to sound disbelieving. 'We wouldn't have gold on our boat. We're not millionaires, you know.' And he attempted to laugh, but even to himself it sounded a little bit thin.

'Well, it looks like gold,' Wilbur said doubtfully.

'I expect it's something to do with getting the keel properly balanced,' Michael said quickly. 'The boatyard probably put weights on when they were painting the bottom last winter.'

Wilbur was obstinately shining the flash on his discovery, and Michael could even see the big screw clamps sticking out to the side.

Michael was running out of ideas. 'Let's ask Peter,' he said, standing up. 'He'll know all about it.'

But Wilbur jumped out of the water on to the bank. 'You're smugglers,' he exclaimed. 'That's what you are. Smugglers!'

'Don't be an ass, Wilbur.'

'O.K. then, we'll ask my Pop. He'll know, right enough. He's in the banking business, and he'll know gold when he sees it.'

'I shouldn't bother,' Michael said, desperately wishing that Peter would appear. 'Nobody would have gold weights on their keel.'

'No,' agreed Wilbur. 'They sure wouldn't. Not unless they were hiding it.' He backed away a little. 'I knew there was something funny about you three,' he said. 'Where are your parents? Why did you say your name was Wilson when Peter told my Pop it was Branxome? I saw the name on Jill's dressing-gown in her cabin – Jill Branxome.' He moved away a little farther as though fearing that Michael would go for him. 'Pop said you were up to something, the way none of you ever say anything about where you've come from or why you're going to Paris.'

'Listen –'

'I'm going to tell him. Then if you can explain what's cooking, well – explain it.' And he dropped the torch and the strainer, turned on his heels and ran off at full speed towards the lock.

'What about the bucket of crayfish?' Michael called in a last effort to hold him back.

But there was no reply. Wilbur did not even look round.

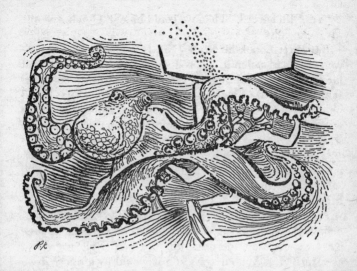

8. What the Squid Did

Michael burst into the cabin where Jill was making up her bunk and Peter was busily sweeping the floor. He poured out the news without pausing for breath. Peter stood up so hurriedly that he banged his head on the ventilator.

'But how on earth did it get there?' Jill stood staring at Michael in astonishment.

'How should I know?'

'It wasn't there at Boulogne,' Peter said, rubbing the top of his head. 'I know, because I would have felt it or seen it or something when I was cutting away the rope that got stuck.'

'We haven't time to worry now about how it got there,' said Michael. 'Jill will have to dive under and get it up before Wilbur is back with his father.'

'Yes,' Jill agreed. 'Then we could hide it. Quick, give me my swim-suit.'

But Peter Shook his head. 'No. It would look as though we really had stolen it. There's nothing to be done but wait for the Tuckers and then see what they do. If they try to get the police on to us we can get a message to Dad. He could be down here in a couple of hours or so, and the letter we wrote from Dieppe would prove that we haven't stolen the stuff.'

'Let's send for Daddy right away,' Jill said. 'There's no need to wait till the Tuckers fetch the police.'

'Or we could fetch the police ourselves,' suggested Michael.

Peter disagreed. 'No,' he said. 'We must keep calm and behave quite naturally. We'll all go out on the bank and see what we can see underneath the boat. After all, we're just as surprised as Wilbur was, and it would look queer if we acted as though we weren't.'

Outside they had not long to wait. As they lay on the grass, peering beneath the hull, Jill saw out of the corner of her eye that Wilbur and his father were already crossing the lock. Shirley was not with them.

'Here they come,' she said. 'We can't just lie here like this. It looks stupid. Let's act normally.'

Peter gave a sour laugh. 'All right then, let's act normally. But what would we do?'

'We should be surprised,' Jill suggested.

'Don't worry. We are.'

'I still can't see how the bars got there,' Michael said. 'Somebody must have planted them on us, and if you ask me it was the Tuckers.'

'Couldn't be,' Peter said shortly. 'We've seen them day and night all the time. Anyway, I think it would look best if we got up and went to meet them.'

They rose to their feet and walked in silence down the path, Peter in front and Jill and Michael a short way behind. Mr Tucker was striding towards them and his pyjama trousers showed under the turn-ups of his flannels. He had put on a jacket too over his pyjama top. Wilbur followed a few yards behind him.

Peter steeled himself for the meeting, and cleared his throat. The American looked business-like and stern, and any cheery greetings would have been out of place. Peter walked on until Mr Tucker was only a few yards away, and then he stopped to let him come up.

'Wilbur's perfectly right,' he said, launching straight in. 'It is gold on our keel. At least, it looks like it. Two bars of it, unless of course there's more hidden farther forward which we haven't seen.'

The effect of this blank statement was to cause Mr Tucker not to brush straight past as he had intended. He slowed his step, and stopped in front of Peter. By the way he hesitated it was clear that he had prepared what he was going to say, but that Peter had taken the wind out of his sails. Wilbur held back awkwardly behind his father.

Peter seized his opportunity and decided to take a desperate risk. 'I'm pretty sure what gold it is too. It's part of the Chesterfield bullion which was stolen in the rail hold-up in England some time ago.' He paused for a moment to let this sink in. 'Come and have a look,' he added after a second or two. And he turned, inviting Mr Tucker to proceed along the path.

There was a strained atmosphere as the party gathered beside the *Dabchick*. Michael and Jill stood a little to one side and Wilbur to the other. None of them spoke to each other, nor to Mr Tucker and Peter as they knelt on the grass at the water's edge. Peter rolled up his sleeve and plunged his arm in with the torch, and although it shone only dimly under the hull its beam was bright enough to be reflected golden from the metal on the keel.

'We'll see if there's any more,' Peter said. He edged sideways along the bank, shining the light towards the keel until he reached the bows. But neither he nor Mr Tucker could see any more precious cargo.

The American stood up before Peter.

'I guess it's my duty to hear your explanation and then call the police,' he said stiffly. He avoided Peter's eye and spoke more to the ground than to anyone in particular. Then suddenly his voice relaxed. 'I sure am sorry it should turn out this way, Peter, after all you've done for us. Let's go aboard and hear what you have to say – unless you would rather not say anything.'

'We'll tell you all we know,' Peter said. 'And then if you want to fetch the police you can. We had nearly sent for them ourselves an hour ago.' He led the way on board. 'Wilbur can come too, and Michael and Jill,' he added. 'They may be able to help.'

When they were all seated round the table, Peter began. 'It goes back to the robbery of the train carrying the American bullion to London in June. The Chesterfield gold was stolen. You'll have heard about that?'

'Sure.' Mr Tucker's voice was still formal and stand-offish.

Peter paused for a moment. He still wasn't absolutely certain that the Tuckers were not somehow involved in the robbery, so he decided to say nothing about Michael having been to the scene of the crime, or his father being in charge of investigations. All that could wait.

'The bullion was in bars, marked with Robert G. Chesterfield's monogram,' he continued. 'At least, that is what was reported in the English papers,' he added quickly, in case Mr Tucker should wonder how he knew. 'The next thing that happened was that you were stuck in the Somme estuary.'

'What's that got to do with it?' Mr Tucker shifted impatiently on the seat.

'Jill can tell you,' Peter replied calmly. 'Come on, Jill, tell them what happened.'

Jill told her part of the tale quite quickly. Wilbur listened in astonishment, staring at her as she spoke. His father watched her too, and, although it was clear that he was intrigued by what she said, it did not look as though he believed it.

'So you're trying to tell me there's gold on our bottom too,' he said when she had finished. 'Well, if there is, how is it that Wilbur didn't see it when we were high and dry a couple of hours back?'

'Because it's not there any longer,' Michael put in.

Mr Tucker shook his head. 'I suppose the fairies took it.'

'They may have done,' said Michael, unable to suppress a giggle. 'Or it might have been the water babies.'

Peter glared at him disapprovingly.

'But if you don't believe it, go and look at your keel,' Michael continued. 'The clamps must have been screwed up pretty tight. You'll see the marks where they were. I saw them myself this morning.'

The American looked at Michael doubtfully. 'Go on,' he said to Peter.

'Well, we decided to shadow you and see what happened,' Peter said. 'And though you didn't know it, we watched the *Marguerite* day and night, at every moment. That's all there is to tell you, except that early this morning when we rowed up past your boat with Wilbur we noticed the bars had gone. About half an hour later Wilbur and Michael found them on our keel.'

'I found them,' Wilbur contradicted.

'Well, you don't suppose I would have let you creep along under the side of the boat, or have shone the light under it if I had known the gold was there,' said Michael quickly.

This made sense, and Mr Tucker was clearly puzzled. 'I still don't understand it,' he said eventually.

'Nor do we,' Peter said. 'But we believe the gold on our keel is the same that was on yours. I'll tell you why.' And he explained how he knew that the keel was free from hidden cargo as far as Boulogne.

Suddenly Michael leapt to his feet. 'I've got it! I've got it' It was the squid, the flat fish, the shark or whatever it was!' he cried.

The rest stared at him. 'So it wasn't the fairies, it was a squid or a shark, was it?' Mr Tucker's voice was sarcastic.

'Yes,' answered Michael excitedly. 'But not a real one.'

'Come on, Michael. Tell us what you're talking about,' Peter said. He did not speak severely, because he knew that Michael's bright ideas, however crazy they sounded, had a strange way of being right.

'Listen. You remember the grocery man who rowed out in the dinghy? What was the very first thing he asked you?'

'It was whether we wanted wines and spirits and a whole lot of other things,' Jill said.

'No it wasn't,' Peter corrected. 'He asked if we were going to Paris, and we said yes.'

'Good!' Michael clapped his hands. 'And then he asked Mr Tucker if the *Marguerite* was going to Paris, and he said no, they were making for Cherbourg. That's right, isn't it?'

'Yes,' admitted the American. 'He did ask us that.'

'And it was only after supper that you changed your plans. Don't you see?'

'No,' said Mr Tucker, 'I don't.' And nor did anybody else.

'It's obvious,' Michael declared impatiently. 'Somebody wants to smuggle gold to Paris. Everything is searched in England, even boats – *but not their bottoms*. So the gold is clamped on yachts leaving wherever it was you came from and when the boats turn up in France, somebody asks them if they're going to Paris. If so, all well and good. But if not, then the gold is taken off and put on somebody else's. That's why the grocery man asked where we were going.'

'By Jove, Michael, I believe you could be right,' said Peter slowly. 'It would explain everything, except just this. How was the gold moved from the *Marguerite* to us? The chandler couldn't have done it.'

'I know. But when I was fishing in the night I hooked something big. I told you so, but you wouldn't believe me. It was as big as a man, and it moved slowly, not like a fish at all. That's what I meant by a squid, because I never imagined it really was a man. Not then, anyway. I told Wilbur about it, didn't I, Wilbur?'

'Yes,' Wilbur agreed. He was silently embarrassed to have raised a suspicion which each moment was appearing to be less well founded.

'It *was* a man, I'm sure,' Michael said. 'A frogman, or somebody with one of these breathing-tube things. It bubbled, anyway. He must have been shifting the gold from you to us, and he fouled my fishing-line and got hooked up. It may have been the grocer, or it may not, but I'm sure that's what was happening.' Michael jumped up and down with excitement. 'I actually had him on the line for a while. It would have been super if I could only have landed him.'

Peter wondered why Michael had not said more about his night adventure at Le Havre before, but he didn't want to ask for fear it might look as though Michael had only invented the story just to fool the American. It was Wilbur who first broke the silence.

'What do you say, Pop? It looks kind of different now we've heard what Jill and Michael had to say, doesn't it?'

His father looked at Michael fixedly. Then he turned his gaze upon Jill, who attempted an embarrassed smile. Finally he looked straight at Peter.

'I'm sorry,' he said with a shake of his head. 'It makes sense except for something you've overlooked.' He turned quickly towards Jill. 'Miss Branxome . . .'

'Yes?'

The American nodded. 'Precisely. Miss Branxome – that's what I thought. Then why did you tell me your name was Wilson?'

'Well, er . . .' Jill stopped awkwardly, and looked at Peter.

'So you won't say? Then I'm going to have Wilbur go down to the lock and tell them to call up the police.' He stood up. 'I'm sorry, but there it is.'

But Peter stood up too. 'I can't prevent you,' he said. 'But you've asked a question and we'll give you the answer. Then you can fetch the police if you want to.'

He felt inside his jacket and drew out a leather wallet from the breast-pocket. Folding back the flap he searched inside it and pulled out some pieces of paper with notes about the times of high water at Dover and the French channel ports, a few pale-coloured thin French notes of a hundred or a thousand francs each, a school calendar, and finally a crumpled cutting from a newspaper. This he straightened out and handed to Mr Tucker.

The slip of newspaper gave a brief summary of known facts about the Micheldever train robbery, but it was the last sentence which was important. 'Chief-superintendent Branxome of the Flying Squad has been put in charge of the further inquiries,' it read.

'That's my father,' said Peter, pointing at the sentence. 'Jill and Michael thought you might get the wind up if they gave their right name.'

'We thought you would think we were shadowing you,' added Michael. 'And we were.'

'Why should I believe that this Chief-superintendent Branxome is anything to do with you?' Mr Tucker looked straight at Peter. 'You yourself told me Branxome is a common English name.'

'That was just in case you were suspicious,' Peter tried to explain, though he realized that it all sounded a bit thin.

Mr Tucker considered. There was another awkward silence as he sat staring at the table, trying to make up his mind. Peter looked at Jill, but she was watching Wilbur's father anxiously.

After what seemed an age he stood up again. 'I think I'll go and have them fetch the police,' he said, avoiding the eyes of the *Dabchick*'s crew. 'It's better that way. I don't care to have us mixed up in this kind of business.' And he moved towards the companion-ladder.

But Peter barred his way. 'If you do, you'll have plenty of explaining to do,' he said with as firm a voice as he could muster. 'Just as much as we shall.'

Suddenly Jill interposed. 'Look here,' she said. 'I've an idea. Let's all go down to the lock and telephone the Paris police and Daddy, saying what's happened. Then if they want to come and ask us any details, they can.'

'I suppose we could phone at this hour of the morning,' Peter said. 'But Dad wouldn't be at the Sûreté, so there wouldn't be much point. Still, we could send a wire, and he would find it as soon as he got there after breakfast.'

'Good idea,' Michael agreed. 'And we could ask Daddy to send a message to the next lock telling us whether to go straight on or not.'

Peter nodded. 'Yes, we could do that. We could wait there until we have an answer, which shouldn't take long.'

Common sense told Mr Tucker that if the *Dabchick*'s crew were really prepared to summon the police they had nothing to fear, and that they could hardly be smugglers. He looked at Wilbur, then nodded his assent.

Quickly Michael rummaged for some paper, and, after a good deal of starting and crossing out and starting again, a message was drawn up.

The American wanted the telegram to state clearly that there was gold on the *Dabchick*'s keel, but Peter shook his head. 'If somebody in the local post office starts gossiping, the thieves may get to hear, and change their tactics,' he said.

'Send it in code,' Michael suggested.

'We can't. We haven't a code book.'

'Couldn't we work up a message with international code flag signs? We've got those in the *Almanac*,' Jill said.

'We might. But I doubt if there are signs for finding gold on your keel,' Peter replied sarcastically.

'I've got it!' Michael cried. 'We can use what-do-you-call-its. Sort of crossword puzzle clues with quotations and things.'

'What on earth are you talking about?'

Michael was not to be put off. 'You write what you want to say, and then I'll code it. You'll see.'

'All right,' agreed Peter hesitantly. 'We'll draw up the message first and then see what you can do to it.'

By the time the telegram had been written and converted into Michael's clue-code it was long and wordy, but Mr Tucker disposed of Michael's fears about the cost by saying that he would pay for it himself. He and Wilbur sat and waited impatiently until the finished article was produced.

Jill read it out.

'Chief-superintendent Branxome of Scotland Yard, Préfecture de Police, 13 Boulevard du Palais, Paris IV. What all that glitters is not was discovered this morning on our canal across northern . . .

'That's a bit vague,' Peter interrupted.

'Vague! I don't get it at all,' objected Mr Tucker.

'Put "canal across er . . ."'

'Schleswig-Holstein,' said Jill. 'We did it in geography last year.' She altered the sentence with her pencil.

'Wait a minute, wait a minute,' said Mr Tucker. 'This is the Seine in France, not a canal in Germany.'

Michael giggled. 'We know that,' he said. 'But it's a clue. Don't you see?'

'Can't say I do.'

'Kiel,' explained Jill. 'Kiel Canal. Keel of the boat.'

'That's clever,' said Wilbur, but his father did not seem so sure.

'O.K.,' he said. 'Go on. Let's have the rest.'

'I suppose you know what "all that glitters is not" is?' Michael asked.

'That might be a bit easy,' Peter interrupted. 'Better put "nor all that glisters" – you know, it's about Gray's favourite cat. It got drowned in the goldfish-bowl. He pinched it from Shakespeare.'

'What's a man pinching Shakespeare's cat got to do with it?' Mr Tucker was thoroughly confused.

'Nothing,' laughed Michael. 'It was Gray's cat, anyway. It means gold. "Nor all that glisters, *gold*."'

'Give us the rest, Jill,' Peter said.

' "What nor all that glisters is not was discovered this morning on our canal across Schleswig-Holstein by the little boy who sings for his supper. Could be the same two things that nor make a cage that were on the things that go with bibs. Chief supper singer wants to tell people whose lot is not a happy one. Both craft will wait for orders at Ecluse de Notre-Dame de la Garenne. Please hurry. P. J. and M." '

'In other words,' Michael translated, 'gold was discovered this morning on our keel by little Tommy Tucker – that's you, Wilbur. Could be the same two bars that were on the Tuckers. Mr Tucker wants to tell the police. And then the bit about waiting at the next lock, which isn't in code at all.'

'Nobody in the post-office will understand any of it,' said Peter.

'What makes you think your father will?' Mr Tucker seemed very doubtful. 'I couldn't figure it out in a month.'

'Oh, but Daddy could,' Michael declared confidently. 'It's easy. He'll understand it the moment he sees it.'

Once the decision to inform Peter's father had been taken, everybody felt better. And just as Mr Tucker was finally convinced that the *Dabchick* party really had no intentional part in carrying bars of the Chesterfield bullion up the Seine, so too Peter finally made up his mind that the Tuckers could not be crooks either. He had already acquitted Wilbur and Shirley, but he had remained undecided about their father right up until now. At last, however, he was sure that Michael's solution not only made sense but was almost certainly a correct explanation of the events. Somehow the gold had been put on the *Marguerite* without the American knowing anything about it, and it had been transferred to the *Dabchick* after Mr Tucker had told the chandler that they were not bound for Paris but for Cherbourg.

Yet the difficult atmosphere created by the mutual suspicion proved hard to dispel entirely, and Jill wisely suggested that they should all go off together to send off the telegram. As Mr Tucker wanted to dress himself first she suggested that they should collect Shirley as well. This was a good idea.

Shirley had not been present during the discussions on board, and her natural friendliness helped to dispel the remains of unpleasantness.

The lock-keeper had just arrived on duty and was filling the pen ready for up-coming barges. He did not seem anxious to let them send a telegram over his telephone, but he explained to Jill that there was a post-office in the village not far away, so they crossed over the weir to the hamlet of Poses behind the trees on the opposite bank.

The man in the post-house was far from pleased to be roused before proper opening time, but Mr Tucker soothed him with a gift of cigarettes whilst Jill explained that the message was important. Peter was relieved to find that the clerk obviously could not understand a word of the telegram itself.

'Well, I guess that's fixed it,' said Mr Tucker as they trooped out of the post-house. 'Now let's forget it. I'm sorry if I treated you rough this morning, but at first sight things looked pretty bad. Perhaps I shouldn't have suspected you.'

'Why not?' Michael replied. 'After all, we suspected you.'

'And you still do?'

'Well, perhaps not. No, on the whole I think we don't,' Michael answered cautiously.

'And that goes for us too,' said Mr Tucker. 'Which means we can have breakfast. I could do with some.'

'Me too,' said Wilbur.

'Then we'll all have it together on the *Dabchick*,' Jill suggested. 'Shirley and I can get it ready while the rest of you bring up the *Marguerite*. It looks as though they're going to make the lock open before long.'

'Can we have the crayfish for breakfast?' Michael asked.

'If you'll let me get busy on them I can make a real good dish of them,' Shirley said. 'And I promise you it will be worth waiting for.'

The morning was bright and warm when at last the two craft continued their way up the winding course of the great

river. On the port hand the chalky downs rose up steeply
from the edge of the water, sometimes with sheer white cliffs
too steep even to hold grass.

It was half-past twelve before the lock at Notre-Dame de
la Garenne came into sight.

'I wonder if Dad is here,' Peter said, scanning the lock
sides ahead. 'I hope he hadn't flown back to England before
our message arrived.'

Michael held back in midstream behind a long barge-
train, waiting for the flashing signal to change from red to
green. The *Marguerite* drew in close beside.

'This is it,' called Peter. 'As soon as we're in we'll go up
to the lock-house and see if there's any message.'

But there was no need to. They had no sooner followed
the barges into the largest pen than a voice called down to
them in English from the quay above

'Throw up the rope. I'll tie it on for you.'

Michael started. Looking up he saw a burly individual in
a tweed suit and trilby hat standing on the edge of the lock.
He might have been just a tourist, but Michael recognized
him immediately.

'Why, it's Sergeant Denby!' he whispered to Peter and
Jill. 'You know – the man who was with the gold in the
railway van.'

Jill flung up the lines, and Denby made them fast before
descending the ladder. He nodded cheerfully to Michael as
he stepped over the deck, and, as soon as he had reached
the wheelhouse and Peter and Jill had joined him there, he
closed the door.

'I've orders from the chief-superintendent to come up to
Paris with you, just in case there's any funny business,' he
said. 'Not that it's likely,' he added reassuringly. 'But you've
come upon the only clue we've got as to how the gold is
brought over, and we mean to make the most of it. Somebody will get that stuff off your boat when you get into Paris
and we're not taking any chances. Here, I've a letter for you
from your father.'

Peter took the envelope, tore it open, and read the letter out loud.

DEAR PETER,

Well done, all of you. You've found how the gold gets over, when all the customs officers in Britain had failed.

Your American friends are all right. The photos were excellent and the Sûreté radioed them to New York. The father is a senior official in the Bank of Pennsylvania with a fine record. The Yard have checked their story and there's no doubt about it. They booked the *Marguerite* months before the gold was even shipped from the States.

Come straight on up to Paris. Just act quite normally and tie up along with the other yachts in the yacht port at the Place de la Concorde. You can't possibly miss it, but it is between the fourth and fifth bridges after the Eiffel Tower.

Don't stop anywhere else on the way up, not even for shopping. You will have to tie up for the night on the way, and to make it quite impossible for anybody to get at the gold during the dark the police have arranged for you to spend the night inside the small lock at Carrières-sous-Poissy, about fifty miles up from where you are now.

As the Tuckers know about the bullion, we have to take them into our confidence to avoid the news leaking out. Denby has a note for them from me, and a covering letter from the American embassy here, asking them to co-operate. They are to come up with you all the way as though they know nothing.

See you in Paris soon – but not just when you arrive. And congratulations on what you've done.

Your affectionate,
DAD.

PS. – The Sûréte people were foxed by your message, but thought it an excellent idea for a code when I showed them what it meant. Who thought it up?

'I say!' Michael exclaimed. 'Isn't it super? It ought to be great fun when somebody tries to get the gold off us.'

'Everything will be ready for 'em,' said Denby. 'They won't get away with it a second time, I can tell you. And now, if you'll excuse me, I had better deliver my messages to the *Marguerite*.'

'Right,' Peter agreed. 'We'll go over, and I'll introduce you.'

'How about lunch?' Jill asked. 'Surely we can stop for lunch as soon as we're out of the lock.'

Peter shook his head. 'No. We'll have to have it as we go. We can't take any chances. Dad says no stopping.'

He climbed up to the quayside and down the next ladder to the deck of the *Marguerite*, with Denby following. Mr Tucker was already at the bottom of the ladder to meet them as they stepped aboard, but Shirley stayed at the bows to tighten in the line as the water rose in the lock. She waved to Peter as he reached the deck, and if she was smiling as she turned away again it was just because she had not doubted for one moment that Peter's explanation about the gold was true. She trusted him instinctively, and because she had been so absolutely sure that she was not mistaken she had refused to go along with her father and Wilbur to tackle the *Dabchick* party earlier in the morning. She was not the least surprised to see a man turn up at this lock in answer to Peter's telegram. She had known all along that everything would be all right.

Wilbur too stayed where he was, at the stern, but when Peter and Denby arrived aboard he seemed to be too busy with the rope even to nod to them. He was just a bit disappointed that the Branxomes' story was now turning out to be true. It was a pity to stumble on something so exciting as the gold on the *Dabchick*'s keel as he had done, only to find that the obvious clue was the wrong one. It wasn't exactly that he wanted the Branxomes to be crooks; Wilbur was sure that Michael couldn't be, because he liked Michael – and anyway, fishing and crooks didn't go together. Jill and Peter were all right too, even if Peter was a bit serious. But somehow it just seemed a little disappointing that things were turning out as Peter had said, and not as he himself had thought they would when he had run back along the bank to tell his father what he had found.

F

Peter introduced the sergeant, and Mr Tucker shook him vigorously by the hand. Although the dispatch of the telegram had seemed to clear up the misunderstanding, and although Mr Tucker had told himself over and over again that the tale the *Dabchick* party told was true, yet all the way up river from Poses odd little traces of suspicion had kept coming back into his mind. He had desperately hoped that somebody would appear at the next lock in answer to Peter's message, but he had not been convinced that it would happen. Now, however, this broad-shouldered man was there in front of him, holding out his wallet with the C.I.D. identity pass under the transparent cover. Mr Tucker was tremendously relieved.

'Pleased to meet you,' he said. And he certainly meant it.

In the wheelhouse Denby pulled out the packet he had brought with him, and Mr Tucker read through the two letters quickly. Then he folded them and stuffed them in his pocket.

'You can rely on me,' he said to Denby. 'Anything that I can do – just say the word.' Then he put his hand on Peter's shoulder. 'We'll stick by you, Peter, don't worry. And when we've seen this business through – why, we'll have a fine time together in Paris.'

The lock was nearly full, so Peter returned to the *Dabchick*, but Mr Tucker insisted that Denby should stay on the *Marguerite* until the next lock farther up, so that Shirley and Wilbur could meet him. As he followed out behind the *Dabchick* he called the two of them into the wheelhouse.

Denby was not a talkative man and he had been trained never to say more than was necessary about any case in which he was involved, but he could hardly refuse to answer Wilbur's questions. He soon discovered, too, that the Tuckers knew practically the whole story, so there was no harm in filling in the gaps. As he did so, Wilbur's first resentment died away, and he soon found it fine to be sitting there talking to a real detective, and even finer to be mixed up in an important affair like this one. He was glad it had turned out that way after all.

'So you reckon they'll try to get the gold off Peter's boat when she moors up in Paris?' asked Mr Tucker when Denby came to the end of his tale.

'I hope so, sir.'

'Then we ought to catch them on the job,' Wilbur said.

'Is there anything special we can do?' Shirley asked.

'Well, miss, we're up against a clever lot, no doubt about that. We don't really know what to expect. I'm sorry you've got mixed up in this at all, and so is the chief-superintendent.'

'I'm not sorry,' said Shirley. 'I'm glad. I want to help.'

'I can make myself useful if it comes to a spot of trouble,' said her father.

'Me too,' said Wilbur.

The two boats were making good time up the Seine. The banks on one side were thickly wooded, and on the other the cliffs fell almost sheer to the water. Here and there they passed a hamlet, and once they ran below a huge ruined castle of grey stone perched on a sharp spur jutting out from the hillside. It certainly was a pity not to be allowed to stop in such a lovely section of the river, but there was no halting even for a moment except at the locks, where Jill and Shirley managed to buy supplies of bread and milk and vegetables. There were only a few locks, but it took an hour or more to pass each one on account of the slow manoeuvring of the great trains of coal barges drawn by the long-funnelled tugs. Tea-time brought Méricourt lock in sight – the second one up from Notre-Dame de la Garenne. Then came Mézy, a couple of hours farther up, and at last, just before sunset, the lock where they were to spend the night. The signal lights were set at red, but they changed to green as the gates of the smaller pen swung back when the *Dabchick* and *Marguerite* came in sight.

The *Dabchick*'s crew had still had no proper night's sleep since leaving Boulogne, and although Peter said that Michael might fish from the lock-gates he was for once too tired even for that. Wilbur too was sleepy after his crayfish hunt of the previous night, and so after supper together they all took advantage of Denby's offer to keep watch by himself throughout the night, and by half-past nine everybody else was sound asleep.

A couple of miles above the lock the River Oise joined the Seine, and as they passed the confluence next morning they found the water changed to an inky black, seething with bubbling scum. Flies rose from the surface, and a horrible smell of dank decay hung over the river. There was much more traffic, too, for the Oise was part of the route for barge traffic from Paris to the coalfields of northern France, and the channel ports of Calais and Dunkirk.

The hills and woods were gone, and in their place came power stations and refineries, coal depots and foundries. Everybody was glad when at last the drab industrial river with its factories and dirtstrewn banks put on a more respectable air as the centre of the great city came closer.

A massive double-decked bridge with a row of rounded and almost Roman arches and a lower layer of broad stone spans bearing the great imperial N of Napoleon marked the beginning of the city itself, with its boulevards and walks, and the embankments stretching ahead on either side to each successive bridge. The *Dabchick* took the centre arch, and Wilbur, who had drawn nearly level, took the next one across to leave plenty of room.

'Pont du Jour,' said Peter. 'Four miles to go, and I'm not sorry it's no farther.'

Michael took a fresh chart, a river chart of the city itself. 'Nine more bridges, I make it,' he counted. 'Five to the Eiffel Tower, and four more.'

'I wonder what will happen when we get there,' thought Jill aloud.

'You don't need to worry, miss,' Sergeant Denby said. 'You'll be perfectly safe. If I were you I would just walk out into the town this evening, all three of you and your friends too. Behave quite naturally, just as you would if you knew nothing about what's down below. I should advise you to do that and leave things to us.'

'What! And let the police have all the fun? I want to see what happens,' Michael exclaimed.

'I'm not frightened,' Jill said firmly. 'I want to stay.'

'I think Sergeant Denby is right,' said Peter in a rather grown-up way. 'You and Michael can go to a cinema or something. I'll stay behind and help him keep watch.'

'If you stay, I'm staying too,' Jill declared. 'It was I who found the gold originally, and I'm not going to be pushed off to the cinema.'

'Nor am I,' Michael said. 'Besides, I think it would look pretty fishy if we cleared off and left the boat with Sergeant Denby, even if Peter was with him. It would be more natural if we were all together. Don't you think so, Sergeant Denby?'

'Well, I don't see why you shouldn't stay,' he admitted.

'And Daddy would have said if he hadn't wanted us to,' said Jill persuasively.

'All right then,' Peter agreed rather reluctantly. 'Only for goodness' sake don't do anything silly.'

Jill ignored the suggestion. 'Is there anything special we ought not to do?'

'No, miss,' the sergeant replied. 'Except just this. If anybody asks you how long you'll be staying, tell them you're moving on tomorrow above Paris, but you haven't yet decided how far you're going.'

'Nor which way,' Michael added. 'If we were really going any farther we might go right up the Seine, and we could turn left into the Marne, or turn right into the Yonne farther up. I've looked it up on the map.'

'And there's the Loing canal too,' said Peter, flicking over the sheets of the map. 'So there are plenty of different routes we could take if we really wanted to.'

'But what exactly do you expect to happen?' Jill asked.

'Well, miss, I can't rightly say. But there's no doubt at all that somebody will come to collect the gold, and what with it being below water there's only one way to get at it, and that's with a diver.'

'Or a frogman, like at Le Havre,' Michael put in.

'That's more than likely,' Denby agreed.

'I've got an idea,' Michael exclaimed. 'I nearly caught the one at Le Havre with an eel-line. Couldn't we hang down lots of lines all round the boat, with millions of hooks on?'

'Honestly, Michael, you are a donkey,' laughed Peter.

Sergeant Denby laughed too. 'Maybe we could,' he said. 'But we don't want to catch him.'

'Why on earth not?' Michael asked, disappointed.

'Because we're not just after recovering these two bars. We want to find out where they are taken to. When he has collected them, the chap must come out of the water somewhere, and that's what we want to discover. It's all in the hands of the French police – with your father helping as far as he can, though he doesn't know the city like they do.'

They were running close past the flight of steps which led from the water's edge up to the gigantic legs of the Eiffel Tower. Inside one of the legs a lift car was crawling up between the girders, and far up against the sky the heads of people could be made out leaning over the balcony rail.

'Gosh,' said Michael. 'It's huge! I hope we can go up before we leave Paris.'

'I had thought of lots of things I wanted to do in Paris,' Jill said. 'Only thinking about the gold I had almost forgotten about them.'

'I might be wrong,' said Sergeant Denby slowly. 'But I shouldn't be surprised if you'll be free to go anywhere you want by breakfast-time tomorrow.'

Peter ran under the central arch of the Pont de Jena, opposite the tower. 'Four more bridges and we'll be there, ready for anything. I hope you're right, and something turns up tonight.'

Round the gradual bend to starboard the final reach came into view and soon the *Dabchick* ran under the great single span of the last bridge. Tall columns stood at each corner, crowned with huge great gilt flying horses with wings outstretched. Cars and dumpy green buses roared across the river in the busy torrent of rush-hour traffic, and beyond the bridge a group of miscellaneous private boats lay dotted along a broad cobbled quay. Over to the left the traffic surged round the great space of the Place de la Concorde.

Peter glanced over his shoulder at the *Marguerite* as she followed up behind, and he eased down to let a big trip steamer pass before swinging over towards the quay. A man who was busy scraping down the varnish on the wheelhouse of a converted fishing-boat laid down his scraper and sandpaper and gave a friendly wave, pointing to the vacant space behind his own craft.

'I expect he's a crook,' said Michael.

'I don't see why you should think anybody is a crook who just tries to be helpful,' Jill said.

'I bet he is, though,' Michael declared. 'You'll see. He'll come up and ask us how long we're staying.'

He went out on deck with Jill to handle the ropes and Peter slid the *Dabchick* gently over to touch against the quayside.

'Bien!' The Frenchman took the end of the line which Jill tossed to him, and stepping on the quay he dropped it over a bollard. 'It is good here,' he said. 'Not too much of the noise, no? And the yacht port, he has a guardian who will watch during the day if you go in the city.'

'Thank you,' Jill said. 'It looks lovely here.' She stepped ashore to help Michael moor the stern. 'There you are,' she said to him. 'You're wrong. He never asked anything about us at all. He was just being helpful.'

9. Statue of Liberty

'Behave naturally, behave naturally, just as though nothing had happened or was going to happen,' murmured Peter. 'It's all very well, but what would we do if we were behaving naturally?'

'Go out into the town,' said Jill sensibly.

'Perhaps nothing is going to happen after all,' Michael said.

'Well, nobody has come and asked us how long we're staying,' mused Peter. 'I thought at least that somebody would come down to the quay and start chatting with us, but they don't seem to be paying the slightest attention.'

'Let's join the others and go for a walk,' Jill urged.

'I don't suppose we ought to leave the boat unguarded,' Michael said.

'Denby said we could go,' Peter advised. 'He's just gone up to report to Dad. He said he would be back in an hour or so, but we were just to behave quite naturally and go off if we felt like it.'

'Then let's,' said Jill. 'Come on. After all, we're in Paris on holiday. Perhaps we've dreamed all this story about bullion. Anyway, let's try to forget it for this evening. We'll see what Shirley and Wilbur want to do.'

At Shirley's suggestion they all strolled together along the length of the broad avenue which led up to the Arc de Triomphe. The time seemed to drag by very slowly, and although Jill and Shirley spun out the minutes by looking at the summer frocks in the windows of all the shops, the evening seemed interminably long. Even the snack supper at an open-air table on the pavement did little to make the time pass more quickly, and though everybody urged Michael to order his long-promised dish of snails he preferred not to do so.

'I'm not hungry, really,' he said. 'Perhaps tomorrow will be different. I'll certainly have them one day, don't worry.'

Wilbur was as unsettled as the rest. 'We'd better be getting back, Pop,' he said, looking for the hundredth time at his watch. 'It's half-past eight, and soon it will be getting dark.'

Mr Tucker had just summoned the waiter for the bill, when a black saloon car which was cruising slowly along the edge of the boulevard came to a halt opposite them. The door opened, a man got out, and the car drove off up the avenue.

'It's Daddy!' Michael exclaimed excitedly.

'I thought I would find you somewhere up here,' said his father after Jill had introduced him to their companions.

'Where's Mummy?' Jill asked. 'Is she in Paris?'

'Not yet. She's coming over next Monday.'

'That's good,' said Peter. 'Then we can all be together again.'

'Yes,' said Mr Branxome. 'And we'll have a fine time if everything's finished by then. You've certainly done a grand job up to now.'

He drew an envelope out of his pocket and pulled from it some official police sheets on which were pasted the photographs which Michael had taken at Dieppe. He pushed them over to Mr Tucker.

'I'm sorry that the young detectives suspected you,' he said with a smile.

Mr Tucker gasped. 'You mean to say you sent those snaps to the police?' He stared at Michael in good-humoured surprise.

'Yes,' Michael giggled. 'We posted them straight off at Dieppe. And there's something else you don't know either, but under my bunk I've got a tumbler with your fingerprints on it. I suppose we shan't need it now.'

Mr Tucker told the chief-superintendent how helpful Jill and her brothers had been in the Somme Bay. 'I don't know how to thank them,' he said.

'I don't know how to thank you for running into the net,' Mr Branxome replied. 'If you hadn't done that, we might never have found out what we have. Still, we can't sit here all night talking. We've work to do, and I wanted to ask if I could come aboard the *Marguerite* for the night.' He explained that he wished to be close at hand, but that an extra man aboard the *Dabchick* might arouse suspicion.

'Why, sure. You're welcome. Anything we can do, just ask and it's yours.'

'Then we had better go, right away.'

And so at last the night drew in, and shortly after ten o'clock the lights went out in the *Dabchick* and a little later in the *Marguerite* too. Wilbur was in his bunk, fully dressed, and so was Shirley. They had been warned not to move in the boat or even to whisper, but the tension of waiting for the unknown was so keen that, although not a sound came from inside the boat, both Wilbur and Shirley were as wide awake as were their father and Mr Branxome, where they sat in silence in the darkness of the wheelhouse.

Aboard the *Dabchick* the crew of three were gathered in the forward cabin, Peter and Michael peering hopefully through the cracks between the window edges and the curtains whilst Jill sat on one of the bunks and strained her ears for the slightest unusual sound. Denby was in the after-cabin, lying flat on the floor with his head propped on his hands above the open bilge. He had removed the trap in the floor, hoping that he would be able to detect any faint scraping or knocking on the keel just below.

Up till midnight there seemed to be little decrease in the noise of traffic rumbling over the bridge near by, but soon afterwards the lights of the city began to go out and the last buses stopped running. Occasional cars could still be heard in the avenues leading to the Place de la Concorde, but they too became less frequent, and a warm stillness descended over the river.

A loud plop close to the side of the boat made a tingle run over Michael's scalp. Jill stood up silently at the sound, but Peter reassured her in a quiet whisper.

'Only a fish.' And he pointed out at the circle of ripples.

Silence fell again, and the ticking of the saloon clock seemed so astonishingly loud that Jill wondered she had never noticed it before. The strain of listening was becoming heavy, and, although she could not have gone to sleep if she had wanted to, she found herself yawning.

'Only one proper night's sleep in the last six,' she thought to herself. 'Yet I'm not sleepy even now – just tired.'

Suddenly the peace of the night was shattered by a blood-curdling yell, a kind of scream of pain blended with rage. Even Peter felt his nerves tremble at the shock of the sound, but he knew what it was.

'Cat,' he whispered. And as though to confirm what he had said there was a light thump on the deck and the sound of paws walking softly towards the stern before the creature jumped back on to the quay again.

'Scrounging, I expect,' Michael whispered. 'Cats always do.'

' 'Sh! We shouldn't be talking.'

A distant bell eventually sounded two o'clock. 'They'll have to hurry,' Peter thought. 'It begins to get light about four.'

The next sound was a muffled movement inside the boat. Tiptoeing through in his stockinged feet Denby's form appeared in the doorway.

'It's gone,' he whispered. 'I heard the chap working on the keel. He's away now. Where are your navigation lights? I said I would give a flash to alert the men on the banks ahead if our visitor came.'

'Here. Come with me.' Almost unsteady with excitement Peter stealthily climbed the steps to the wheelhouse, with Denby close behind. He silently opened the lid of the instrument panel and pointed at a knob in the dim grey light. 'That one. Pull it up for on.'

'Give him another few seconds,' Denby said. 'We don't want him to see the lights and take fright.' He counted softly to himself and then reached over to the knob. 'Right!'

It was only a dim glow from the small white light above the wheelhouse, but in the blackness of the surroundings it was enough to show something which made Peter start. In the stern well of the fishing-smack immediately in front of their bows a man was leaning over the side. He was pulling at a dark black shape which stretched upward from the water to the gunwale above.

Denby saw it in the same instant, and hurriedly switched off the light again. 'Did you see . . .?'

'Yes,' whispered Peter. 'But what was it?'

'A black man being hauled aboard. He must be the chap we're after, and here right under our noses.'

'What shall we do? Shall I slip off and fetch my father?'

'No. Better stay here as though we saw nothing. There's no reason why they should suspect us. If we lie low they'll probably wait a bit and then slip out into the town and lead us to the place we want.'

But Mr Branxome had seen the signal from the *Dabchick*,

and he was already hurrying up the quay. Quite unaware that the boat just ahead was involved, he jumped on to the *Dabchick*'s deck and pulled open the wheelhouse door.

'Nice work, Denby,' he called. 'So they're away with the gold, are they?'

Neither Denby nor Peter had time to answer before the engine of the fishing-smack started.

'Quick, sir! They're off.'

Followed by Denby and Peter, Mr Branxome stumbled over the deck and jumped for the quay to race for the fishing-boat berth. But they were too late. Already she was well out from the side and drawing out astern into the stream. Hopefully Denby grabbed one of the mooring ropes, but it lay slack, dangling in the water below. It had simply been slipped.

'After them, Peter,' his father shouted. 'I'll get the *Marguerite* to chase them too.' And he ran off down the quayside towards the bridge.

Denby had another idea. Neck and neck with Peter he tumbled on to the *Dabchick*'s deck, and as the smack's stern swung past in the dark he leapt outward with all his strength from the edge of the deck. It was a noble effort, but the distance was too great for anybody but a champion jumper, and he fell short with a heavy splash.

'Michael, Jill,' Peter yelled. And as they stumbled out on deck he gave rapid orders. 'Denby's in the water. Get the rope ladder down at the bows. Quick! We've got to go after them.'

'It *was* the fishing-boat,' Michael exclaimed excitedly as he ran to the bows. 'I knew the man was a crook. I said so, didn't I?'

'Yes,' admitted Jill. 'But it was only a guess, and he might not have been.'

Peter had darted below to make his way through to the fuel tank in the stern, to turn on the petrol. Forgetting that Denby had lifted out the floor trap in the after-cabin he tripped over it and fell into the bilge. A collection of cast-iron

ballast blocks was not the most pleasant bed in which to
land head first, but Peter had no time even to consider his
bruises or the oily fluid on his trousers. He scrambled out
again, opened the door under the stern counter and turned
the cock.

By the time he was back on deck Denby was being hauled
over the edge of the catwalk, dripping and panting but more
determined than ever for the chase.

'Throw off the ropes; shove her out,' Peter shouted. And
racing into the wheelhouse he pressed the starter and the
engine roared.

'Right away,' called Jill from the stern, and Peter put the
engine full-speed ahead, swinging the wheel slowly to clear
her from the quay.

'Which way?' he shouted.

'Down through the bridge,' Denby called. 'I can hear
them.'

'Hang on, everybody.' Peter spun the wheel right over,
and the *Dabchick* heeled with the force of the turning. He
switched on the navigation lights, then put them off again.
Better to give as little clue as possible to their position, he
decided.

'Sit down,' he called out. 'Sit down. I can't see ahead for
the bridge. Michael!'

'Yes?'

Michael ran back and joined his brother. So did Jill.

'You take her, Michael. You've got cat's eyes, and I'm
going to be ready to board them with Sergeant Denby if we
can catch them.' Peter handed over control of the ship and
ran forward.

Michael stood straight behind the wheel, staring ahead
through the windshield and over the heads of Peter and
Sergeant Denby where they squatted low on the fore-deck
to give him a clear view.

'Poor Denby,' said Jill. 'He always seems to be getting
into trouble.'

'I thought you were going to say getting into hot water,'

laughed Michael. 'And I don't think the Seine can be very hot at this time of night.'

'But what happened?'

'I don't know. But we're to chase the fishing-boat anyway.' He felt the throttle control and made sure that the *Dabchick* was running as fast as she could. 'Look! There it is!' He pointed a little to port and Jill could just make out the white gleam of the wash round the fishing-boat's stern. She was perhaps a couple of hundred yards ahead as the *Dabchick* shot the arch of the first bridge.

'Hooray!' Jill clapped her hands. 'And here comes the *Marguerite* too!' The white hull of the American's boat was just drawing out from beside the quay.

'I wonder who's handling her,' Michael said. 'I hope it's Wilbur. He's mustard on steering.'

'So is Shirley,' said Jill.

'I think Wilbur's best. Next bridge coming up.'

'Can you see?'

'Yes. I'll take the second arch from the left.'

Jill held her breath as Michael roared under the roadway of the Pont des Invalides. 'I don't think we're gaining,' she said as the echo died away. 'Why don't the police do something?'

'They'll have a police boat out somewhere, I expect,' Michael said. 'Even if they haven't, that boat can't get away. It's only about ten miles down to the first lock. They've got to do something before they get there, or they've had it.'

Meanwhile the *Marguerite* was gathering speed and just holding on to the chase a hundred yards or more astern. Wilbur was indeed at the wheel, and he cut over to take a different arch from Michael so that the slipstream of the *Dabchick* would not cut a fraction off his speed.

'D'you think we'll catch them, Mr Branxome?' he asked.

'We've got to. It was most unfortunate that they cut away and ran for it, because they are our only clue. We've got to catch them.'

'We're running full speed,' Wilbur said. 'I can't see them at all.'

'I can,' said Shirley. 'Look. They're just there, by the bridge beyond the next one.'

'Keep going, Wilbur,' his father said. 'Keep going.'

The fishing-boat was still holding its own, and sweeping through the Pont d'Iéna it ran up towards the next bridge, the Pont de Passy. This and the next two bridges were connected down the centre of the stream by a long low island with tree-lined walks, and the Allée des Cygnes, and Michael saw the faint form of the smack moving over to take the left-hand section of the river. He turned the wheel to follow, and then he had a better idea.

'We'll take the right hand. I think we'll make on them.' And he altered course for the right arch of the Pont de Passy.

Peter yelled back towards the wheelhouse. 'They've gone the other way,' he called. 'Over to the left.'

Michael shouted back. 'I know, but this is shorter. I think we'll gain.' He held to his decision and ran past the spit of the island on the opposite side to the smack. 'Honestly, I can't think why they haven't got a police launch out by now,' he said. 'Still, I don't really want the police to catch them, and I hope they don't.'

'You hope they don't? Why on earth?' Jill was puzzled.

'I want us to catch them. I don't want other people to come interfering at the last moment.'

'I don't mind who catches them, so long as Daddy finds out where they take the gold,' Jill said.

Aboard the *Marguerite* Michael's choice of the opposite channel had been seen, and Wilbur was doubtful which way to take.

'Michael's gone the wrong way,' said Mr Branxome with a frown. 'He must have lost sight of them somehow. We'll have to carry on by ourselves. Run down to the left, Wilbur.'

The *Marguerite* kept over towards the left bank, still just holding the fishing-boat in view whenever the bridge lights reflected on the water ahead showed up its dark form.

'Silly of Michael, really,' said his father. 'It's up to us, now. It's our last chance. Every blessed thing seems to have gone wrong tonight. I suppose I ought to have known that the chaps might be in the yacht harbour, and now that they've taken fright we'll never find where they deliver the goods.'

'I think we're gaining,' Shirley said, trying to sound cheerful.

'We're not falling behind, anyway,' agreed Mr Tucker. 'But she's got a good turn of speed, that craft.'

Meanwhile behind the island Michael was running straight down the channel, straining his eyes for the bridge arches.

'Right a bit,' Jill called. Then, 'No, left. I can see straight through the centre arch.'

They were just passing under the railway span, and Michael too could make out ahead the three arches of the Pont de Grenelle between the tip of the island and the right bank.

'I'll take the left one. It's straighter,' he said.

The *Dabchick* was making her top speed of just under eight knots, and Michael was confident that, with choosing the opposite channel to the fishing-boat and thus being free of its wash, he would gain at least a few yards. Peter and Denby peered ahead through the bridge, hoping to see the smack run out into the river beyond the island, but there was no sign of it.

'We're doing pretty well,' Peter declared excitedly. 'They're not out yet, so we must have gained on them quite a bit. With any luck we'll be able to draw up on them and get aboard.' He crouched beside the rail with Denby, ready to spring when the chance came.

Denby felt hampered by the weight of his wet clothes, and he took off his heavy jacket and laid it in a sodden heap on the deck.

'Leave this to me, Master Peter,' he said. 'It's not your business to get mixed up with fellows like these. It's different for us – we know how to look after ourselves.'

'I can look after myself too,' said Peter. 'Besides, you may need help, and Michael can manage the boat. If you're jumping, so am I.'

'I don't think your father would want you to,' Denby reasoned.

'Well, we haven't time to stop and ask him, I'm afraid,' said Peter with a short laugh. He jumped quickly to his feet, and so did Denby.

'What on earth . . .'

Just as Michael was shooting the arch a dim black shape emerged from behind the point, heading right into the same bridge hole.

'Look out, Michael,' Peter shouted. 'Look out!'

Whether the runaways realized or not that there were two craft chasing them, they were certainly unaware that the pursuit was not following straight in their course, and they had evidently decided to try to escape by doubling back round the island. The two men aboard her were certainly just as astonished as Michael to find themselves racing for the arch with another boat surging down in the opposite direction. Almost instinctively Michael threw the engine astern and switched on the spotlight, and as the *Dabchick* trembled and shook with the reversal of her propeller the fishing-boat swung right over away from the bridge. Her stern swept past only a few feet from the *Dabchick*'s bows, and for a moment Peter and Denby seemed about to try a leap, but they were not quite close enough.

There was still plenty of way on the *Dabchick*, and Michael wheeled hard over to the right, narrowly missing the massive pier of the arch as he shot out of the bridge. But in the split second of decision he had chosen wisely, for the runaways had lost speed through their own double turn, and, putting the engine ahead again, Michael was able to run up almost level of them on the outside.

'Close her, close her!' yelled Peter. And he too stripped his jacket to be ready to fling himself aboard.

But the smack had no intention of giving up so easily, and

her steersman carried his swing right round to turn the point of the island once more into the channel down which he had just come. This left the *Dabchick* with the longer course on the outside of the bend, and put at least a little distance between the two craft.

Right beneath the great statue of Liberty with her lamp held high in her hand, the smack clipped round the stone bull-nose of the island, straight in front of the oncoming *Marguerite*.

Mr Branxome snatched the *Marguerite*'s wheel as the boat appeared immediately beyond the bridge. Deliberately he headed her straight for their quarry. He was not going to let them escape a second time.

'Hold on. Get down, away from the glass,' he ordered quietly.

In the couple of seconds that remained, the smack had no time to avoid the other ship, and with a rending crash the *Marguerite*'s bows ploughed into her amidships, pinning her against the wall where the lawns of the island sloped down to the water just above the bridge. There was a deafening noise of shattering crockery as once more the *Marguerite*'s lockers emptied themselves with the shock. Mr Branxome was thrown forward across the wheel, and Shirley was flung against her father, who lurched sideways against the front of the wheelhouse, splintering the windshield into fragments.

Just as they were picking themselves up, the *Dabchick*'s spotlight swept round on the scene. 'Quick,' yelled Peter. In its gleam two figures could be seen racing up the bank and disappearing among the trees.

'Confound it,' said Denby. 'They're away.'

'Oh no, they aren't,' said Peter abruptly as he ran to the wheelhouse, grabbed the wheel and twisted it towards the island.

'Peter . . .' Michael saw only the fishing-boat ahead, with the *Marguerite*'s bows embedded deep in her planking. 'Peter, look out!'

Jill clutched the edge of the chart table as Peter burst

through the doorway again, staggered up on to the top of the wheelhouse and sprang. A second later, as Michael wrenched the wheel to starboard to avoid crashing into the two craft Denby also jumped. This time he managed to reach the wall, and he fell forward on to the grass, but in a flash he was on his feet again, racing after Peter between the bushes and along the gravelled walk of the Allée des Cygnes.

The chief-superintendent was first out of the *Marguerite*'s wheelhouse. He ran forward, scrambled on to the deck of the fishing-boat and over on to the bank with Mr Tucker close behind him. They too raced across the flower-beds and under the trees, and the American swore as he fell full length over a rose bush.

Panting, Denby pulled out his whistle and blew as he ran, and an answering blast came from a policeman somewhere on the shore away to the right.

'This way,' Peter called. 'There they are!' He could hear the gravel scattering as the men fled up the walk, and in the dim light of the night he thought he could see something moving.

An electric train roared noisily over the viaduct which crossed the island half-way along its length. Still running Peter glanced over his shoulder but he had already out-distanced Denby, and he did not know that his father and the American had also joined the chase. He heard Denby blowing his whistle again, and this time there was a repeated shrill answering call from somewhere straight ahead.

When the rumble of the train died away into the tunnel Peter could no longer hear the sound of running on the gravel ahead. Fearful that he should lose his quarry he ran on with every extra ounce of energy he could muster.

He had almost reached the upper end of the island when something hard struck him on the head as he ran close past a dark clump of shrubs. Half-dazed, he faltered, stumbled and fell.

Immediately Michael saw Peter and Denby jump on to

the bank he put the engine full astern to avoid crashing into the two entangled boats. The *Dabchick* was very close inshore, and it was only the work of a few moments to bring her in against the wall. Almost before Jill had fetched up a line from the lockers, Wilbur and Shirley were ready on the bank to take the rope and tie it round a tree. Then the *Marguerite* was made fast, to stop her drifting down-stream with the fishing-boat still impaled on her nose.

Michael switched off, and jumped ashore with Jill. In the light of their spot-lamp they saw that Wilbur's face had blood on it.

'Are you all right?' Jill asked, putting her arm round him.

'It's nothing,' he replied with an attempt at a smile. 'I just hit my nose when we crashed them.'

Michael pulled out his handkerchief and dipped it at the water's edge for Jill to wipe away the blood.

'He's O.K.,' Shirley said. 'His nose always bleeds.'

'Do you think they've got them?' Wilbur asked.

'They'll catch them, all right, I expect,' Michael said. 'Only things have gone wrong. Daddy wanted to follow them and see where they took the gold, but they got wind of it. I don't think Sergeant Denby had any idea they were on the boat in front of us when he flashed the lights on.'

'Gold!' Wilbur exclaimed suddenly. 'The two bars off your boat should be here.'

'Of course,' said Jill. 'I had forgotten that.'

'Then let's get them.'

'Be careful, Wilbur,' said Shirley as her brother jumped on to the fishing-boat. 'She might sink.'

'Yes, she must be pretty badly holed,' Michael agreed.

'I'll go and get my flash,' said Wilbur. 'Then we'll see.'

Gingerly they all four stepped into the stern of the fishing craft, with Wilbur leading and shining his torch on the floor. Farther forward under the deck portion they could hear the sound of water pouring through the shattered side, and Wilbur shone his beam in through the door. Where the floor dipped down it was already under several inches of water, but they quickly saw what they were seeking. Shining bright and clear just inside the doorway were the two bars of bullion.

Wilbur managed to heave them up, and very carefully they were passed back and placed upon the bank, well away from the edge of the water.

Suddenly Michael had an idea. 'If we can keep the boat afloat we might get salvage money,' he said quickly. 'If people abandon a boat and you stop it sinking, then they have to pay you. It's sometimes as much as half what the boat's worth.'

'Not outside tidal waters,' Wilbur said. 'And I guess the police will get hold of this one, anyway. Still, we should stop her going down, salvage money or no salvage money. How do we set about it?'

'Stuff up the hole with cushions and blankets – that's what they say in yachting books, anyway.'

'I'll throw some over,' said Shirley. 'Better use ours, and not spoil yours. I guess the *Marguerite* may be out of commission for a while.'

'Oh, I don't think so,' Michael said. 'She took it head on. She should be all right.'

'Why use your bedding things? Use theirs,' said Jill. 'There's plenty of stuff lying about.'

'They won't be needing it either,' laughed Michael. 'I expect French prisons provide their customers with bedding.'

Michael and Wilbur took off their shoes and socks and rammed the bedding into the hole as Jill and Shirley pushed at the *Marguerite*'s bows to clear her out of the side of the boat. The flow increased at first where the *Marguerite* had blocked it, but soon the two boys had it reasonably under control, though they were soaked through in the process.

'There,' said Wilbur as he pushed and squeezed a final seat-cushion into the torn side. 'That's fine. And if we can pump her and bring her up a bit the hole will be above water anyway.'

'Good idea,' Jill agreed from outside. 'We can bail with buckets. I'll get some.'

Before long they had the water down to floor level, taking it in turn to fill the buckets and hand them outside, or to lift them and tip them over the edge.

'She's nearly dry now,' said Shirley at last, pausing for breath.

'If we lift up the floor-boards and bail the bilge she will be,' Michael said.

'O.K.,' Wilbur agreed. 'Then here goes.' Holding the torch in his teeth he reached down for the ring in the loose section of the cabin flooring, and heaved. And as the trap came up he opened his mouth with a startled cry and the flash-lamp fell into the bilge and broke.

The bilge was full of gold.

'Sure you're keeping count?' Michael panted as he dragged out another bar to Jill, who passed it up the bank to where Shirley was laying out the haul in rows on the grass.

'Ninety-one,' said Jill.

'I made it ninety-three.' Wilbur straightened his back, stiff with bending down into the bilge.

'It is, with the first two,' Shirley agreed. 'I've counted them too.'

'Here's another.' Wilbur hauled up a bar from the forward corner of the floor space.

'Ninety-four. And it's just beginning to get light,' said Jill. 'Then we'll see better.'

'No sign of the others,' Shirley said, stepping over to the walk and staring up towards the opposite end of the island. 'Guess they must have had some chase. We've been here an hour, maybe more.'

'How many bars were there?' Wilbur was crouching in the bilge with the water round his knees.

'A hundred and four,' Michael said. 'Only we don't know that it's all been brought over yet.'

'Ten to find,' said Wilbur, feeling once more over the ribs and stringers in the bottom of the hull.

'Only seven, or even less,' Michael corrected him. "They've already picked up three in Paris, and perhaps more. Daddy will know.'

'Well, there's enough here to be going on with,' laughed Jill.

The faint sound of distant movements on the gravel path made Shirley turn round.

'It must be them,' she said. 'That you, Pop?' she called out.

'Yes, we're coming,' came her father's voice.

The others joined her, and together they stood peering up the walk in the faint light until they could make out the figures of Mr Tucker and Mr Branxome. Then they ran forward to meet them.

'Have you got them, Daddy?' Jill called as they approached.

'No,' he said. 'I'm afraid we're back where we started, and we've lost our only clue.' He sounded angry.

'But they couldn't have got away, surely,' said Michael. 'Where's Peter?'

Mr Branxome gave a sour laugh. 'The police here are certainly keen,' he said. 'The first thing they did was to collar Peter. A chap hit him with a truncheon as he ran up the walk near the far end. A couple more sprang out on Denby, and though he knocked one of them out the other blew his whistle and some more came off the bridge and overpowered him.'

'When we ran into them, they attacked us too,' explained Mr Tucker, fingering a torn collar and tie. 'Unfortunately we didn't know what to say in French, and they had the handcuffs on us quick as lightning.'

'I know what to say in English,' growled Mr Branxome. 'And by Jove I'm going to say it too, when I get back to the Préfecture. The blasted idiots.'

'Is Peter all right?' Shirley's voice was anxious.

'Yes, he's not hurt really. He and Denby are just being tidied up at the police station, and then they're coming down here with the inspector. The place will be crawling with police in a few minutes, now that it's all over.'

'What happened to the fellows you were chasing after?' Wilbur asked.

'Goodness knows. They probably just hid among the bushes while the police carted us off. They must have had a good laugh. Then I expect they just walked away as safe as saints while we were being shut up in a cell at the police station. We would still be there if an inspector hadn't turned up who recognized me.'

'The police have sure messed this business up badly,' said Mr Tucker. 'We could have got those fellows in another couple of minutes.'

'I'm not so worried about losing the men,' the chief-superintendent growled. 'It's the Chesterfield gold I'm after, and we nearly had our hands on it. This has finished it. We can't expect them to ship any more up the Seine the same way.'

Michael nudged Jill. Then he whispered something to Wilbur and Shirley, and put his fingers to his lips.

'I suppose that back at the Yard they'll think you've slipped up badly,' he said. 'It's such a pity. You so nearly got the gold, but not quite. And we tried so hard to help, didn't we?'

'Sure,' said Wilbur. 'It's too bad you lost it this way. Maybe you should have left it to us to go after it.'

'Of course there might be a couple of pieces in the fishing-boat,' Jill suggested. 'You know, the ones that were on our keel. That would be better than nothing. You wouldn't have to go back to London quite empty-handed.'

Mr Branxome looked angrily around him. Then suddenly his face relaxed as he recognized the particular furtive smiles which Jill and Michael always wore when they were pulling his leg.

'Great Scott!' he cried. 'Do you mean ...? Have you ...?'

Jill nodded and took his arm. 'Wilbur found it all under the floor. Come and see.'

'Under the floor! Why didn't I guess –'

'I can't imagine,' said Michael. 'After all, before we ever left England I told you that if I wanted to hide the gold I would put it in a boat, in the bilge.'

And so the Chesterfield gold was found. Four more bars came to light in the forepeak of the fishing-smack and a further two were found by a police diver on the bottom of a Dutch yacht which arrived at the Place de la Concorde next day. Of the hundred and four bars, all but one were accounted for, and that one bar was never traced. Perhaps it was stolen by the chandler who shifted the bullion from keel to keel in Le Havre, but he never admitted it. Nor for that matter did he ever admit having been in any way connected with the robbery, and, as the only evidence against him was Michael's fishing adventure at night, the police could not make a charge. After all, as the chandler said with a polite smile, it really might have been some large and rare fish which Michael hooked.

Though all but one bar was found, nobody realized better than Mr Branxome that if the *Dabchick* had sailed from England even one day later the whole lot might have disappeared, for the bars found on the Tucker's craft and later transferred to the *Dabchick* were the last but two to be shipped up the Seine on unsuspecting yachts.

'Which all goes to show that you should never wait for better weather, or you might miss something,' said Peter.

'And you should keep your eyes open too,' Michael added. 'If we hadn't been curious about why the *Marguerite* was stuck off the Somme entrance we would never have known about the gold.'

'All the same, I think it proves something different,' Jill put in. 'You remember we all suspected the Tuckers –'

'I wouldn't say that,' said Peter.

'Oh, wouldn't you. Well, you did, anyway. Just because you like them now you can't pretend you didn't think they were crooks.'

'Well, it looked as though they were,' said Michael.

'I know. That's the point. It just shows that you shouldn't always judge people by first appearances, however bad things may look. There's always a chance you may be wrong.'

'Thanks,' said Peter with a laugh. 'I wish you had come up the path on that island with me, and said all that to the policeman who hit me on the head. You could have said it all in French too.'

Who placed the gold aboard ships in the Hamble river was never discovered, nor where it was previously hidden, but the two men who led the *Dabchick* and the *Marguerite* on the great chase down the Seine at night were caught hiding in the railway tunnel where the line from the viaduct over the Allée des Cygnes plunged down towards the Gare des Invalides. One – the man with the scraper and sandpaper – turned out to be a receiver of stolen property who had eluded the police for several years. The other, who still had the remains of the black grease-paint round his ears, was not really dark-skinned at all. He was a young swimming-bath attendant who had foolishly let himself be persuaded to dive under the boats for ten thousand francs a time. But it is doubtful whether he ever got his money.

As for the fishing-smack, she was repaired at a slipway in Paris and eventually sold by the police to a fisherman at Boulogne. He gave her a name as well as a number, and called her the *Cache d'Or*. She often fished round the banks off the mouth of the Somme, and in fine weather she occasionally crossed to the English coast and set her nets a few miles off shore. The holiday crowds on the Channel packets hardly noticed her as they ran by, bound for the Continent, and certainly none of them ever wondered how she came by her unusual name.

When work began on the Hemming Memorial Hospital for Sick Children, Mr Robert G. Chesterfield of Pittsburgh sent a gift of the value of the one bar never recovered, but this time he sent it by cheque.

Peter and Jill and Michael were present at the ceremony when the foundation stone was laid. They had received special invitations. Just after the mayor had tapped the stone into position and laid down his trowel he asked them to step forward, and, opening a wooden case, he drew out two packages which he handed to Jill. The first and larger one contained the ship's bell of the fishing-smack, newly engraved with the words:

'With the compliments of the Prefect of Police, Paris.'

The second parcel was quite small, and when Jill had opened it she held up a tiny model in gold of a woman in a long gown holding a torch high in her right hand, and a book in her left.

For a moment Jill was puzzled. Then suddenly she recognized it as the statue of Liberty, beneath which they had worked away to unload the bullion from the bilge of the fishing-smack.

'La Liberté éclairant le Monde,' she read on its pedestal.

'Why it's just like it too,' she exclaimed, holding the little statue on the palm of her hand. 'It's absolutely lovely. But . . .'

She looked at Michael and Peter, and the three of them whispered together hurriedly before Jill spoke once more to the mayor.

'Do you think we might give one of them to some friends of ours in America who were with us? You see, the gold would never have been found without them.'

'I think you could,' he said, looking from one to the other. 'If you're sure you really want to.'

'Yes, we do,' said Peter.

'The only question is, which they would like,' said Jill, as she picked up the bell and looked at it.

'If you don't mind my making a suggestion, I should send them the bell,' said the mayor, as he shook Jill's hand. 'I believe they've got one of those statues in the United States already. Only it's rather a different size.'

Roger Pilkington is well known for the delightful books which have come from his many years of voyaging through the waterways of Europe. But he enjoys writing for young people best of all because, he says, they appreciate much better than grown-ups the excitements and adventures of real life.

He and his wife and their two children spend their holidays exploring on their own small boat *Commodore*, usually with other young people aboard as well, and his gay and informative accounts of their travels appear in the 'Small Boat' series.